A BILLIONAIRE'S TREASURE

AN ALPHA BILLIONAIRE ROMANCE

MICHELLE LOVE

HOT AND STEAMY ROMANCE

CONTENTS

About the Author	vii
Synopsis	ix
Blurb	xi
A Billionaire's Treasure	1
1. Lola	3
2. Arsen	8
3. Lola	12
4. Arsen	19
5. Lola	25
A Billionaire's Possession	33
6. Lola	35
7. Arsen	43
8. Lola	46
9. Arsen	51
10. Lola	56
11. Arsen	65
12. Lola	68
13. Arsen	70
A Billionaire's Troubles	73
14. Arsen	75
15. Lola	81
16. Arsen	89
17. Lola	93
18. Arsen	101
A Billionaire's Strength	105
19. Lola	107
20. Arsen	117
21. Lola	120
22. Arsen	123

23. Lola	131
24. Lola	147
25. Arsen	154
26. Lola	156
27. Arsen	162
28. Lola	167
29. Arsen	169
30. Lola	171
31. Arsen	173
A Billionaire's Fate	177
32. Lola	179
33. Arsen	181
34. Lola	184
35. Arsen	189
36. Lola	192
37. Arsen	195
Sign Up to Receive Free Books	207
Preview of The Surgeon's Secrets	209
Chapter 1	211
Chapter 2	216
Chapter 3	224
Chapter 4	228
Other Books By This Author	237
About the Author	239
Copyright	241

Made in "The United States" by:

Michelle Love

© Copyright 2020 – Michelle Love

ISBN: 978-1-64808-054-8

ALL RIGHTS RESERVED. No part of this publication may be reproduced or transmitted in any form whatsoever, electronic, or mechanical, including photocopying, recording, or by any informational storage or retrieval system without express written, dated and signed permission from the author

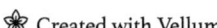 Created with Vellum

ABOUT THE AUTHOR

Mrs. Love writes about smart, sexy women and the hot alpha billionaires who love them. She has found her own happily ever after with her dream husband and adorable 6 and 2 year old kids.
Currently, Michelle is hard at work on the next book in the series, and trying to stay off the Internet.
"Thank you for supporting an indie author. Anything you can do, whether it be writing a review, or even simply telling a fellow reader that you enjoyed this. Thanks

Facebook
facebook.com/HotAndSteamyRomance

Instagram
instagram.com/michellesromance

SYNOPSIS

When he first laid eyes on her, he knew she was the one. She had brown eyes, wavy hair, and plump lips painted a matte wine red. What first caught his eye was the smirk on her face when the teacher called out everyone's name and she didn't reply. As he watched her, he wondered how she could be bold enough to sit in on someone else's class.

He walked to the middle of the class with his hands behind his back and smiled. You could hear the silent whistles and occasional *oh my god* coming from the female students. All except for her. That was new for this charming older man. She didn't even move her eyes up from her bag to see what was going on. The older man was caught off guard since he was always the center of everyone's attention when he walked into the room. A woman had never not taken an interest in him, so this random student not giving him the time of day made him drawn to her and only her.

"Hello, ladies and gentlemen. My name is Arsen Lockhart and here's how I became a billionaire novelist", the man announced before the class. As soon as the word "novelist" slipped out it was as though something clicked inside of her brain. Her head popped up immediately and she began paying attention.

Lola Anderson. She was the epitome of stubbornness and ruination. Her only goal was to become a novelist, so she had never had time for relationships, or even friendships. Except for one, that is. Lola had a best friend named Arabella Spencer and they had had an unbreakable bond since middle school. Lola was currently skipping her eight o'clock math class to spend time with Arabella and never expected that there would be a seminar. Who could have known that this one day would be the start of something interesting?

BLURB

They made eye contact from across the room and from the moment he saw her, he knew he had to have her. She bit down on her lip as she watched the much older man walk around the classroom. It was really a coincidence that on the day she had skipped her class a great opportunity like this came about. There had to be a reason the universe pulled them together.

A BILLIONAIRE'S TREASURE

An Alpha Billionaire Romance

By Michelle Love

1

LOLA

I began to feel very drawn to Arsen as he started his presentation. Despite the fact that I was in college, I hadn't met any other guy who had that certain type of confidence he did. I examined the way he walked, with his back straight and chin up, the way he spoke slowly making sure every word was articulate, and the way his eye contact burned holes straight through anyone's head. He was the perfect guy, if I wanted one.

I quickly shook away the lustful thoughts and started to take notes. He went into detail about how to market your novels for the age group you want to sell to, and that's where I struggled with my work—trying to make someone want my book in their home.

Arsen also owned a line of hotels across the country named after himself, The Lockhart. I wasn't interested in any of that, though. The fact that this man was a novelist was really attractive to me. He told us about his daily routine and how strict he was with time for his employees. It showed how ruthless he was when it came to his work. He was stern and didn't play with his work. He was a man who knew what he wanted and got it. What was this feeling? I fanned myself lightly and continued taking notes.

A half hour went by and the presentation was over. When Arsen went around to hand out his business card for whenever we needed to 'contact him,' his smile melted the hearts of all of the female students. I fell victim to this feeling, but I would never let that be known. When he handed me the card, we made eye contact and there was a tingling feeling throughout my body. He winked and I was taken aback, feeling attracted but confused. I guess he noticed because he chuckled and moved on to the next row of students.

"What was that?" Arabella asked, smiling. "He was totally just flirting with you"

I rolled my eyes and pulled my bag over my shoulder. "You're over-analyzing things, Bella".

"You like him!" Her eyes widened with excitement as she stared at me.

I raised an eyebrow, trying to mask my nervousness, and stood up from my seat. "I need coffee," I forced out and left the room quickly.

I'm not sure how a simple gesture could get me to crack like that, but it was strange, and I had never felt that before. I rushed out of the class and straight to the coffee shop to clear my mind. I started to think about Arsen again as I waited in line. His suit was so nice—form-fitting without a single piece of lint. His hair was so dark and his gray eyes were piercing.

"Hello! What can I get for you?" I heard faintly in my head. That confused me, but I ignored it. "Excuse me!!"

I snapped back into reality and realized the barista was trying to get my attention. I laughed softly. "Sorry about that. One large cup of vanilla hazelnut coffee please".

The barista put in my order, then told me my price. As I looked through my bag for my wallet, I heard a familiar voice.

"I've got it, and add another large coffee. Black" I saw a man extend his arm, handing the barista a black card. Her eyes lit up at the sight of him and my body tensed up. All of my feelings from just ten minutes ago came rushing back when I turned to see Arsen standing next to me with a smirk on his face.

"You didn't," I spoke lightly, then cleared my throat. "You didn't have to."

"I wanted to, so I did." He chuckled and took his coffee from the barista, and I did the same. "Let's talk."

My eyes widened, and he chuckled again and walked away to a table in the corner. Taking a deep breath, I followed him to the table and sat in front of him.

"You're not afraid?" I asked.

"Of?" He furrowed his eyebrows.

"Being out in public without some sort of bodyguard or protection. You know ... being a billionaire and all." I took a sip of my coffee and almost moaned as the warm liquid rushed down through my chest.

"I have nothing to be scared of ..." He trailed off, not knowing my name.

"Lola," I stated simply and stuck my hand out to shake his. He grabbed my hand and placed a kiss on it. I heard a girl gasp from the table behind us and I rolled my eyes.

"Too much?" He asked, referring to the kiss.

I shook my head in disagreement. "Girls here are just annoying sometimes, but why did you want to speak with me?"

He smiled and took a sip of his coffee. He licked his lips and that made my stomach full of butterflies. "I saw you taking notes and I wanted to ask you what you thought about my seminar."

"Arsen Lockhart cares what I think?" I questioned and smiled lightly.

"I do." He smiled and drank more of his coffee. "So tell me, Lola, what did you think?"

"I really admire how hard-working and dedicated you are." I pushed my hair back behind my ear. "Actually ... can I interview you the next time you're available?"

"Uh. Sure. What will this interview be about?" He leaned back in his seat and crossed his hands.

"You and what made you want to become a novelist." I stared into his eyes as he nodded.

"I should be free next Tuesday around three. I'll tell my assistant. Don't be late, Lola." And with that, he stood from his seat and left.

I just sat there, not knowing what to do really. I was confused about why he decided to leave so abruptly, but after a few minutes, I shook away the thought and went on about my day. I grabbed my cup of coffee and headed back to my suite, which I shared with Anabella. When I got there, she was sitting on the couch waiting for me with a smile on her face.

"Why are you looking at me like that?" I chuckled and took off my jacket, hanging it on the coat rack.

"I saw you and Mr. Lockhart at the coffee shop! You totally have a thing for him, Lo"

I plopped down on the couch beside her and kicked off my shoes. "Why do you think I have a thing for him? We only spoke for like five minutes." I pulled my feet up and looked over at her.

"That's the reason, Lola! You never give any guy—" I cut her off.

"He's not a guy. He's a man. So what if I talked to him? That doesn't mean I like him"

"You never give any guy or man the attention to even have a five-minute conversation. You're a hi-and-bye type of girl" Anabella smiled. "It's good that you say you don't like him because he's too old for you anyway."

Too old? I thought to myself. I'm a grown woman. I can date anyone I want, however old. I mentally rolled my eyes and flashed Anabella a fake, small smile. "Yeah. I guess you're right."

Three days of normal activities went by and it was finally Tuesday. For some reason, I wanted to wear something that would catch his eye, so I decided on a black button down, a black skirt that hugged my waist and hips, and a pair of red heels. I did my makeup neutral with a bold, dark brown lip. I straightened my hair and smiled at myself in the mirror. If this look didn't grab his attention, I didn't know what would.

When I walked out of the bathroom, Anabelle's mouth dropped. "Where are you going? You look so hot!"

"My interview with Arsen is today." I smiled and grabbed my bag from the couch. "See ya' later, babes."

I could feel her watching me in disbelief as I left, but I shrugged it off. As I walked toward my car, a ton of guys looked my way or tried to talk to me, but I only wanted Arsen's attention. I hadn't been interested in a guy since I'd been in college, so the act of developing feelings for someone was new to me. Like learning how to walk again.

I pulled up to his office. It was a place I had always seen, but had never thought to research, since this wasn't the place I was from. When I walked through the huge glass doors, my heels clicked against the marble floors. That sound made me feel bold for some reason and helped me stay focused. I was here for an interview, not to fall into the arms of Arsen Lockhart.

The walls had big, beautiful paintings on each wall. 'The Lockhart' was written on the wall behind the front desk. Although it was a big building, I felt as if I belonged. Like this was the place I needed to be.

2

ARSEN

"He's straight through the doors," I heard my assistant say from afar. I turned from my view of the city to see Lola sitting there, looking as beautiful as ever. I was shocked. She looked completely different from the girl with the jeans, sneakers, and ponytail she'd been when I first saw her. I smirked and sat down at my desk.

"Hi, Mr. Lockhart. How are you today?" She sat in front of me with a smile on her face and her notebook in hand. I watched as she opened it and wrote something down. She looked back up at me, confused as to why I was staring at her, but I just chuckled and leaned back in my chair.

"I'm doing great, Lola. How are you?" I stood and walked to the front of my desk, leaning against it. I looked down at her in her chair and finished before she could speak. "Let me guess ... 'I'm doing well Lockhart, and I'm looking very beautiful as well.'" I mimicked her voice and laughed.

. . .

SHE CLEARED her throat uncomfortably and shifted in her seat. "Good. Um. Actually, Mr. Lockhart, I was going to say I'm doing fine." She looked me directly in the eyes with a straight face.

I LAUGHED. She couldn't possibly be serious right now. Who knew she couldn't take a joke? Scoffing, I grabbed a cigar from my desk and lit it. "Well, what are your questions?"

"FOR ONE, I wanted to know what inspired you to become a novelist." She looked down at her book, ready to write. Her nails were painted beige and her hands looked soothing and slightly glossed from the lotion she had used.

"SINCE I WAS YOUNG, I've loved reading, so by the time I was seventeen, I had written my first book. It was never published, but since then, I've been extremely passionate about writing. It's really all I've ever wanted to do with my life, so I decided to turn it into a career. Now look at me—a billionaire!" I laughed and took a drag from my cigar. I loved talking about myself. It's not so much of a 'cocky' thing to do. I'm just very confident, and talking about myself helps remind me of how I made it to the top on my own.

"Great," She spoke, writing down what I'd just said in her notes. "And how long have you been writing, Mr. Lockhart?"

"TWENTY YEARS." I returned back to my seat. "Published my first book when I was twenty-two years old"

. . .

I saw her eyes widen slightly, but she continued to write. Her bracelets clanked together softly and her hair fell on her face. She was so beautiful. I really wanted her in my life. There was a silence in the room and the air grew thick. I decided to lighten the mood a bit.

"How old are you, Lola?"

"'I'm twenty-one, Mr. Lockhart" She kept her eyes on her notes, but I could see her face turning red.

"Do you want to be a novelist?" I asked and she nodded.

She finally looked up at me and spoke. "I do, Mr. Lockhart"

"Call me Arsen," I told her "How badly do you want to be a novelist? How hard are you willing to work for it? It's not as easy as you may think. You can't just write a book and get it published. It's much more than that. It's hard to catch the reader's eye these days, and this field is competitive, since most people read on their electronics. To get to the top, you have to be the best and don't stop working, ever, until you get what you want."

She sat there in shock, not doing anything. She had

completely stopped writing and just stared at me. She was startled and I could see it all over her face.

"Let me mentor you, Lola." I smiled and leaned forward on my desk.

"O-okay, Mr. Lock—Arsen." She shifted in her chair once more and wrote something down in her book. I could see her begin to turn red in the face again.

"Every Tuesday, same time." I stood up and fixed my tie. "I'll show you out"

She looked at me, confused, and stood up, following me toward the door. Before she could fully exit, I grabbed her hand and planted a kiss on it. She furrowed her eyebrows and continued walking.

I couldn't afford to be around her too long or I might just grab her and kiss her. She was so gorgeous, standing at 5'6 with a perfect curvy figure and long, black hair. Her freckles were like constellations and her lips were pouty and desirable. There was no doubt in my mind that she was the most beautiful girl I'd ever seen in my life, and I had to have her. I didn't mean to come on to her too strongly. I guessed that she just needed time to get comfortable around me. She seemed stubborn about who she gave her attention to and that's what attracted me the most. I'd be a fool to let her slip through my fingertips.

3

LOLA

He did it again! Cutting our meetings off short, as if there wasn´t work that needed to be done. I rolled my eyes at the thought of it and got in my car. I didn't understand him. The interview was going well until he just went on a rampage about what's it was like being a novelist. I appreciated the advice, I really did, but I didn't expect all of that in that very moment. I definitely didn't expect the kiss he left on my hand before I left. Although that was a very interesting experience, I am happy that he asked to be my mentor. I needed someone like him to help me get where I need to be. The only problem with that plan will be trying to focus on my work with him breathing down the side of my neck. I felt like I was going to melt right in his office, but showing extreme amounts of affection too early with a guy can turn him off or give him the leverage to use you.

When I made it back to my suite, I thought of ways to avoid Anabella, but luckily, she wasn't there. All I could do was lie in bed and think of Arsen. I hadn't felt the weight of a crush in years and it made me feel like an irresponsible schoolgirl again. There was just something about the way he talked. His voice almost struck fear into my heart. Those bold eyes and pink lips. That slender body in that dark suit. I felt myself getting hot and breathing heavily, so I had to quickly take my mind off of the thought of him. I rolled over on my side and pulled my laptop onto my bed. I opened it and the last piece of writing I was working on appeared on the screen.

It was titled "Daisies & Apricot." It was a short story I had written about my past lover who always brought me daisies and apricot-scented body scrubs. As I read over it, I thought that I would come across some similarities between my ex-boyfriend and Arsen, to give me a little hint as to why I was so attracted to him, but that wasn't the case. Arsen was the exact opposite. He was challenging. All of my past boyfriends were very sweet and submissive. Their personalities fit so well with my dominate behavior. They all fell to my knees the moment they saw me, but Arsen Lockhart was different. He saw me and felt attracted, but he didn't fall to my knees like the rest of them. He remained strong and determined. That's what attracted me the most about him.

I was so used to being around childish little boys that thought being over the age of eighteen made them "real men," but Arsen was a real man. Strong, hardworking, dedicated, and stern, all while being confident. He had everything he wanted in the palm of his hand and he could control people however he pleased. Except for me, of course. I liked him too, but I wasn't that easy. I was a tough cookie who took a while to be cracked, so if he thought he could have me falling to my knees in a couple of days, he had another thing coming. I smiled, closing my laptop and putting it on my bedside table. I had a man who had my dream job and also had a thing for me. Why not use this to my advantage?

I TOOK one red rose and one white rose from the vase on my desk and carried them to the bathroom with me. I needed some time to relax and to also care for my skin, so I ran a warm bath and added the petals from the roses, pink salt, and a few drops of lavender oil. When I first put a foot in, I felt the warm water kiss my skin and it automatically put me to ease. I played my favorite album on my phone and just relaxed. This was everything that I needed.

I was about three songs in when my phone began to ring. I dried off my hands on a small towel and picked up my phone to see who it was. My eyes widened at the name on the screen. Arsen Lockhart. What was he doing calling me after our meeting? Hopefully it was to tell me why he ended our session so quickly. I hesitated a little, then answered. For some reason, it felt really good to hear his deep voice on the other line.

"HELLO, LOLA," he spoke, not saying anything else.

"HELLO, Arsen. Is there anything I can help you with?"

"I'M TRYING out this new restaurant tonight and I want you to come with me."

. . .

"Well, Mr. Lockhart, I-"

He cut me off. "I'll pay for everything and you can ask me any of the other questions you were going to ask earlier today."

"I guess dinner wouldn't hurt ..." I trailed off and sat up in the tub.

"It wouldn't, so I'll pick you up at 7:30. I'm wearing a navy blue suit, so work around that." And before I could even get a word out, he hung up. I guessed I was going on a date. I sat there genuinely confused and sort of turned on, but I quickly shook off the thought and began to wash off.

When I got back to my room, I looked in my closet and thought to myself, "What do you wear on a date with a billionaire?"

I had to look like arm candy. Arsen Lockhart wouldn't just go out with any girl. It was 6:30, so I just laid out my clothes and started on something else to pass the time. I decided on a simple black dress that hugged my curves, with a pair of heels. I straightened my hair and put on light makeup, but I made sure to wear a bold red lip.

"Where are you going tonight?" I heard Anabella speak from the door.

. . .

"Out," I replied simply.

"Yeah, sure, Lola. Have fun with Mr. Billionaire." She chuckled and walked away. I didn't know what upset her so much about my going out with an older man, but I was a grown woman. If I wanted to date someone much older, I had every right to.

I rolled my eyes at her remark and walked over to the bed to slip on my dress. I felt so beautiful with it on. I never wore it because my mind was too focused on my studies to go on dates. To go anywhere at that. All my life consisted of was writing. I remembered that when I was around eighteen or nineteen, I knew how to balance being a party girl and still getting everything done that I needed to do. That sadly wasn't enough for me, though. I wasn't reaching as much success as I wanted, so I completely cut out partying and having fun at the age of twenty, and here I am today.

I was twenty-one years old and had butterflies before going on a date. There was nothing wrong with that. I just always thought life would turn out differently for me. Maybe that was why I was so open with Arsen. It might not seem like it on his end, but I didn't usually even give guys the time of day, so he was lucky. I felt that he could be that missing excitement that I needed in my life. I was just so used to being by myself without any distractions. I wasn't sure if a relationship was what I needed right now, but I was willing to try it out.

My phone lit up, showing a text from Arsen. It said that he was outside and that his driver was waiting for me. I laughed a little and slid on my shoes. I didn't even know why I expected for a billionaire to drive himself to a restaurant. I made it outside and saw the driver open the back door. I kindly thanked him and got inside. Arsen sat, watching me get in the car with a smile on his face. His teeth were the whitest I'd ever seen. All of his teeth were so perfectly straight that it was mesmerizing.

"You look absolutely stunning," he spoke.

"Thank you. You look good as well, Arsen." I blushed slightly at the nickname he gave me.

The ride there was lovely. I got to see the view of downtown at night, while music played softly in the background. The air was fresh while blowing through my hair. I felt like my nineteen-year-old self again. I heard a chuckle and turned to see Arsen watching me.

"Having fun there?" He smiled.

And for the first time, I actually smiled back. "I am, actually. I'm feeling a bit nostalgic"

"I understand." He nodded. "Go out with me more often and you could feel this all of the time"

The smirk on his face made my stomach drop. "As pleasing as

that offer sounds, I'll have to see how the rest of the night goes before I make a decision"

He shrugged with a smirk on his face and turned to face the window as we pulled up at the front of the restaurant. I waited for the driver to open my door and thanked him after. I looked up at the big, white letters.

"The Crystal Room," Arsen spoke, reading my mind. He grabbed my hand, causing me to tense up and pull my hand away. "It's okay, Lola. I don't bite."

I nodded and he grabbed my hand. "At least not too hard," I heard him mumble as we walked in.

4

ARSEN

I watched as her body moved swiftly in that dress. She was the most gorgeous girl I'd ever laid eyes on. I liked a woman with curves, long hair, and an attitude. I was determined to make her mine.

"Hello, Mr. Lockhart. Your table is this way"

We followed the waitress to our secluded table, upstairs on the balcony and took our seats. I ordered us some wine and watched as she looked over the menu.

"See anything you like?" I asked, raising an eyebrow.

"Not really ..." She closed her menu and sat back in her seat. "Order for me."

. . .

I smirked and looked over at the waitress, who had begun to pour our wine into our glasses. "Are you ready to order, sir?" She smiled down at me.

"We are," Lola stated loudly. The waitress jumped a bit from how stern Lola's voice was and I chuckled. She clearly wasn't expecting for her to be that bold. Lola seemed a bit protective over me, but I liked it.

I scanned my eyes over the menu and decided on what we were having. "We'll both have the steak and lobster dinner with mashed potatoes on the side."

"C-coming right up." The waitress spoke as she collected our menus and walked away.

"Jealous?" I asked Lola as I took a sip of my wine.

"I could never be jealous, sweetheart. Look at me." She smiled and took a sip of her wine as well. "I just don't like being disrespected. I deserve just as much of respect as you do"

That turned me on—the way she thought so highly of herself. I just wanted to tear that little piece of fabric right off, but I had respect for her. A strong, beautiful woman like herself took time and patience, but I was sure I'd get her to crack soon.

"I want to know more about you, Lola. Have you always wanted to be a novelist?" I folded both hands together and leaned back in my seat.

"Since I was about seven, I knew I wanted to write. Every other day I'd try to write a new story or start reading a new book to get inspired. My life literally revolved around it." She took another sip of her wine and licked a drop of it off of her bottom lip.

"There was never anything else you wanted to do?" I raised an eyebrow.

She nodded. "There were, and I did them. I took ballet for a couple of years, I used to sketch, and I'm a pretty amazing cook. I used to want to be a chef as well, but over the years those just became hobbies. I knew I wanted writing to be my career."

"Ballet, huh?" I smiled. "Explains why you have such strong and beautiful legs. I'd love you taste your cooking one day, since you've bragged about your talents"

"You'd be amazed." She smiled and ran her finger around the brim of her glass. "This wine is amazing. So smooth and opulent."

"You want a bottle to take home?" I asked.

. . .

"I sure do." She smiled widely. "Thank you"

Just then the waitress came back with our plates. The food looked absolutely delicious—almost as delicious as Lola. Usually the girls I dated would light up at the expensive meal before them, but it was like she was completely used to this. Has she dated rich, older men before?

I shook the thought and asked the waitress for another bottle to take back home. She politely told me that she'd wrap it up and put it in a bag for us. I nodded and turned my attention back to Lola, who was cutting into her steak. Seeing the fork slide in between her lips after taking a bite made me hot.

"Is the night going well for you?" I asked, staring into her eyes.

"Wonderful," she stated with a smile and continued to eat.

"Maybe we could do this again tomorrow night?"

"Sounds lovely, Arsen, but I'd really like the next time we see each other to be at our next meeting." She poured herself another glass of wine. "I have a lot of work to do and I would love to be undistracted."

"Oh." I cleared my throat. I'd never been turned down. I was starting to wonder if she even liked me. I began eating my food.

"I WOULD LIKE to do this again, though. She smiled and continued eating.

"THEN WE SHALL." I wiped my mouth clean and smirked.

"ARSEN LOCKHART, I am going to murder you!" a woman screamed as she ran towards me. She began hitting me, yelling that I had killed her husband and ruined her family. Lola was shocked, but managed to pull the lady off while workers rushed over to see what all the commotion was. I dialed my driver's number and told him to be out front of the restaurant immediately.

"I'M SO SORRY, MR. LOCKHART!" A random woman said to me as she tried to clean off the food that the woman had spilled on my clothes while going crazy. "I'm the manager and I'm not sure why this would happen"

"YOU SHOULD REALLY WORK on your establishment if you're going to let crazy people like that inside of a place like this." I looked at her, then over at Lola, who was taking the extra bottle of wine from the waitress. I quickly grabbed her free hand and dragged her out of there. We quickly got inside of the car and the driver sped off.

"UM, what was all of that about?" Lola asked.

. . .

"I have no idea. I've never seen that woman a day in my life." I shrugged and turned to look out of the window. I knew exactly who that woman and her husband were, but that was none of her business.

I heard her sigh deeply and adjust herself to face the window. She probably didn't want to go out with me again, but I would make sure that she did.

5

LOLA

That was one of the weirdest things I'd ever encountered, and the fact that Arsen knew absolutely nothing about the situation seemed very fishy to me. I really loved the feeling of being taken out and shown off, but not if things like that were going to be happening. I wondered if he was hiding something.

"Why do you think she'd do that? Throw an entire fit in front of everyone, claiming that she'd want to kill you in a public restaurant, and why would she accuse you of killing her husband?" I unlocked my phone to text Anabella to tell her that I was coming home and that I didn't have my key.

"Simply because I am a billionaire, Lola. People will do anything to get their hands on my money, even if that means accusing me of false crimes. I don't even have the time to kill some random man." He scoffed.

"I guess you're right," I agreed and looked out of the window the entire ride back. When we pulled up to my dorm, I called Anabella, but there was no reply.

"Let me walk you to your door," Arsen offered with a smile.

"No, it's okay. I've got it." I laughed slightly and proceeded to step out of the car, until I felt him pulling me back by my hand.

"What? Do you think I'm going to murder you or something?" He smirked, staring me directly in the eyes, and I felt my body go entirely numb. His voice sounded so chilling—more serious than playful.

"N-no, you can walk me there," I said quickly, pulling my hand away and getting out of the car fully. I was in such a blank state of mind that I forgot to thank the driver.

"Here's your wine," Arsen said walking around the car and handing me the bag. I nodded with a slight smile, then led him into the building and up to my door. I knocked a few times, but there was no answer. I tried calling a few times too, but there was still no answer.

"I mean, you're always welcomed to stay with me for the night," Arsen offered.

There was a solid ten seconds of silence before I even replied. I had to seriously think, *do I really want to stay with this man after he made several romantic advantages or do I want to sleep outside in the hall until Anabella realizes that I'm here*. I turned to him slowly and laughed. "You promise you won't kill me?"

"I'll try not to." He threw his head back and let out a loud chuckle that made me jump. His arm slid around my lower back and he walked me back outside to his car. The car ride back to his place was long and silent. The only sounds were the wind and soft music playing in the background. I felt like something was going to happen tonight, but I just couldn't put my finger on it.

We pulled into the driveway of his house and it was luxurious. I had never seen anything like it before. There were plants everywhere and I could see the view of the pool upon entering. The driver got out and opened our doors, wishing us a good night, and Arsen led me into his home.

"This place is so beautiful." I looked around at the fiery red furniture and black decor.

"Almost as beautiful as you, Lola. Follow me." He led me to the clear doors of his elevator. "Let's get you into something more comfortable."

"What did you have in mind?" I raised an eyebrow.

"Nothing too serious. My daughter is a little younger than you. She comes to visit time from time, so I always have new clothes here for her to sleep in," he laughed. "She's a little smaller than you, but I don't think there's anything that you can't sleep in"

When we made it upstairs, it was just as huge as the downstairs. There was a long marble-floored hallway that led to what I suspected was his bedroom, because it was the biggest. Upon entering, I saw the biggest bed I'd ever seen in my life with black silk sheets.

"Wait here while I go get you something to put on." He winked and then left the room.

I wasn't quite sure how to feel about that. I was just happy to take these shoes off. I sat on the edge of his bed and kicked off my heels. I found a small hair tie in my clutch and pulled my hair into a high ponytail. I looked around the room and it was very minimalistic, but still very opulent.

"I found this for you." Arsen spoke and my head snapped in his direction. He closed the door behind him and walked over to me. He handed me a champagne-colored silk nightgown. He began unbuttoning his shirt and walking into the bathroom attached to his room.

"Where can I change?" I asked him.

"Right there." He peaked his head out of the bathroom. "Don't be afraid. I won't look"

I heard him laugh as I tried to quickly get out of my dress and get into the new one. When I took off my bra, I turned to see him walking out of the bathroom in only his boxers. Let me tell you, for an older man, he had a great body. I erased the dirty thoughts from my mind and just stared at him.

He looked at the shocked expression on my face and down at my body and smirked. I looked down and noticed that I was only in my underwear. The air in the room became thick and I quickly grabbed the gown to cover myself. I didn't have a bad body, but for some reason, I felt really embarrassed and uncomfortable. I mean I'd only known the guy for a couple of days. It wasn't really the right time to be naked around him, especially when I wanted to wait for this moment if things even got that far with Arsen and I.

"Lola, you don't have to hide from me. We're both old enough to be naked around each other and comfortable with it" He walked by me and picked up my clothing from the floor. He placed them on a chair next to his desk and looked over at me again.

"Where will I be sleeping?" I tried changing the subject to take away from the awkwardness.

"With me, hopefully," he responded. "I respect whatever boundaries you have. I just haven't slept next to a beautiful woman in a long time."

I nodded slowly, not wanting to put up a fight, and climbed into bed. He turned off the light and got into bed next to me. Directly across the room was a huge floor-to-ceiling window and the curtains were pulled back completely. There was a beautiful view of not only the moon and stars, but of the city as well. I could see almost every building that was well-lit and that alone made me feel safe. The light from outside made it easier to see around the room and to see that Arsen was staring at me staring at the view.

I looked over at him and smiled. "The view is beautiful. Thanks for letting me experience this"

"Anytime you want to see it, let me know" He ran his hand over my thigh and it drove me crazy. "You know, Lola, I've wanted you ever since I've laid eyes on you"

"I'm well aware, Arsen," I replied bluntly, trying not to say too much.

"Well, do you feel the same way?" I felt him move a little closer to me.

"Maybe." I smirked and rolled over on my side. I felt him pull me back so that my body touched his and his hand grazed my leg.

"So why aren't we doing anything about that?" His hand slipped between my thighs and I began to melt, but I wasn't going to let him know that he had full control of my body at the moment. I pulled his hand away and laughed lightly.

"Goodnight, Arsen Lockhart."

"I really felt like the connection was there. I guess not." He spoke quietly. He moved back away from me and turned over. "Whenever you're ready, Lola, just let me know"

"Again," I smiled to myself. "Goodnight, Arsen Lockhart."

I woke up to a mist of water on my face. "Wake up, angel."

I sat up and rubbed my eyes to see a woman standing over me with a tray of food. "What was that you sprayed on my face? It feels ... really refreshing"

"Rosewater, ma'am. Mr. Lockhart ordered that we wake you up beautifully with a nice breakfast"

"Mmm." I smiled, closing my eyes and inhaling the smell of pancakes. The woman placed the tray of food on my lap and I automatically dug in. It was like nothing I'd ever tasted before, although it was a simple meal—pancakes, eggs, and bacon with a cup of tea and a bowl of fruit on the side.

"Mr. Lockhart had to leave early for work but he says that you are welcomed to stay here until he gets home. He left you an outfit at the end of the bed and if you are ready to leave before he gets home, just let me know and I'll phone the driver" The woman smiled and left the room without saying anything else.

Who would've expected that Arsen would even let me stay after things didn't go as he planned last night? I guessed he really liked me. I sat the tray of food aside after I was finished eating and slid out of bed, grabbing the clothes that were left for me. I walked to the bathroom and saw the most beautiful shower I had ever laid eyes on. The shower head was the entire ceiling and the doors to the shower were clear with a gold trim. I was in love.

I took off my clothes and hopped inside. I turned on the shower and the water fell down on me like the mist of a rainforest. I looked at the shelf built into the shower and saw all of the beautiful bottles of body wash and shampoo. I helped myself to whatever I needed and got myself cleaned up. I grabbed the two folded towels inside and dried my body and my hair.

After taking the best shower of my life, I put on the dark jeans and fitted shirt that he had left me. These really hugged my body, so I guess he picked them out for a reason. I walked back to his room and shot him a text asking if I could check my email on his computer.

While waiting for his reply, I walked around the upstairs of the house and eventually found his daughter's bedroom. She looked just like him, gorgeous and model-like. I saw why her clothes were too tight on me. She looked around seventeen or eighteen. I wondered if she knew her dad liked girls a couple years older than her. I saw a picture of a woman who seemed to be her mom. I wondered what the relationship was like between her and Arsen and why they weren't still together.

I shrugged away the thought and went to explore more of the house, then Arsen finally texted back and told me that I could use the computer. I continued my exploration down the hall and into another room, which was just full of plants and a different computer from the one in his room. For some reason, I felt the urge to use this one.

I sat at the desk and turned it on. To my surprise, there was no password on it. I logged into my email as an extra account because I didn't know if I should just sign out of Arsen's or not. I clicked through a few messages and saw that classes were canceled today, so that was good on my part. I was going to skip them anyways. I really felt tempted to just switch over to Arsen's account and see what an actual novelist's inbox consisted of.

So I did it. I scrolled through a couple of spam messages and emails for upcoming book events until I saw something interesting. A read message was titled, "I am going to kill you, Arsen Lockhart." It reminded me of the crazy woman from the night before, so I decided to open it to see what it was about.

"Dear Arsen Lockhart,

I knew about this whole little business you and your rich friends were running and I had nothing to say about it because it didn't affect me that much, but you have crossed the line. Michael was a kind, loving man and father of three who was just doing what he had to do to provide for his family, and you go off and kill him? He had a life! Whether he had your stupid drug money on time or not, he still had a life and a family and you took all of that away from him. You took him away from us. Now what are we going to do? He was the one who made a living for us. Either you give me 5 million dollars or I am going to kill you, Arsen Lockhart! I will sabotage your entire drug cartel and make your life a living hell!!"

I quickly exited out of the email. My heart was beating extremely fast. I knew Arsen was hiding something by the way he reacted last night, but I didn't know that it was a drug cartel. I didn't know that he would actually kill someone! I shut off the computer and stood up. I turned to leave and saw Arsen standing at the doorway.

"Hello, Lola," He said sternly.

A BILLIONAIRE'S POSSESSION

An Alpha Billionaire Romance

By Michelle Love

6

LOLA

Have you ever felt as if time has stopped around you, but in that specific moment you were unable to move? Unable to think and speak clearly. That's exactly how I felt after learning that the man that I was developing feelings for was a murderer, then turning to see that him watching me go through all of his private information.

My heart dropped to the pit of my stomach as I hesitated to respond to Arsen. He raised an eyebrow with a smirk on his face.

"I see the clothes fit you well," he spoke, looking me up and down.

"Hello, Arsen." I finally managed to speak and looked straight past him into the hallway. "Yes, the clothes fit very well. Thank you"

Before I could even make it to the door, Arsen stepped in and closed it behind him. "Did you ... find all that you were looking for on the computer?"

I gulped and nodded. "I'll just be leaving now."

When I tried to walk past him, he grabbed my wrist and I felt myself being pushed against the wall. I gasped and looked up at Arsen, who was now hovering over me. I could tell by the look on his face that I was caught and this wasn't going to be easy.

"You know, it's really not polite to go through people's emails. You don't have the right," he spat.

"I don't know what you're talking abo—" I mumbled and was quickly cut off.

"Don't play stupid with me, Lola. I was standing in the doorway the entire time," he scoffed.

"Arsen, I swear—" I was cut off again.

"I know what you saw on that computer and you don't know how much trouble you're in now, Lola. But you don't seem like the type to be a loud mouth about these type of things, so I'm considering letting you go." After he said that, I felt so much relief. He smirked down at me and backed away slowly. "Just know that if you run your mouth about anything, you'll end up like that woman's husband. Unlike his situation, your family won't have the fortune of ever finding your body."

That was oddly a turn on. Not the fact that he would kill me, but the way he was so serious. Not once did he crack a hint of a smile. His face showed zero emotion, almost as if he was heartless. No man has ever talked to me in that tone of voice and it gave me a bit of a rush. Feeling myself shake in fear and pleasure, I bit down on my lip and nodded in agreement. He flashed a look of confusion as his eyebrows knitted together. He was clearly confused about my reaction. For once, I felt ...submissive, and I liked it too.

"Come on. I'll give you a ride home. You can grab your things from the bottom of the stairs." He turned and left the room, and I followed after him like a lost puppy shortly after. It seemed as if the hallway grew longer with every step I took. The tension was so heavy and the air was so thick that I found myself almost out of breath. I fanned myself to try to calm down.

Once we made it down the stairs, I grabbed the bag with my things in them and slid on my heels. They surprisingly went well with the outfit I was wearing. I said my goodbyes to the house workers and went outside to Arsen's car. He was already inside, staring forward toward the view of the city.

I realized that this wasn't some bad boy, good girl fantasy. This was real life and I was actually next to a murderer. I never understood how people could kill one another. It just didn't make sense. I guess it could come down to that sometimes, but from what I had read, Arsen was completely in the wrong. If that's how things were in drug cartels, I was glad I had never become a part of one.

I sat in the front seat and as soon as I closed the door, he sped off. I didn't even have time to put on my seatbelt. He must have still been upset about the situation. Why wouldn't he be? Some random girl had found out his biggest secret. I'd be pretty upset too. There was an awkward silence between us.

His grip on the steering wheel made it painful for me to watch. I found myself constantly switching my thoughts. One moment I was thinking about how amazing it felt to be put in my place and another moment I was realizing how my life was actually in danger at that point. I wasn't sure if I actually had an attraction for this side of him or if I was just romanticizing the situation to make myself more comfortable.

I wondered what he was thinking about. Maybe about the ways he would tell his gang that I had found out their secret, or maybe about how I had betrayed him by going through his personal emails. I guessed I would never find out, because I was too afraid that asking him that might just make him snap. I decided to just leave that situation alone and focus on the city lights ahead of me. They brought me some type of peace in this terrifying issue.

Arsen was so deep into his thoughts that he didn't realize that he had passed my building on campus.

"You missed my building." I spoke a little too loudly. He jumped a little and quickly put the car in reverse, moving back toward my building. I admired his tightened jaw and how straight it looked. His skin was very smooth without any wrinkles. I guessed anything was possible when you were a billionaire. I grabbed my bag and opened the door. "See you tomorrow, Mr. Lockhart."

He finally looked at me for the first time since we left his house and raised an eyebrow, questioning my statement. I smirked and stood from his car.

"I'll be at your office to finish my interview with you. Three o'clock, sharp." I spoke with my back turned to him, and before he could respond, I walked away. When I made it to my floor, my door was wide open and Anabella was moving what looked like a few old things from the place. I greeted her with a simple hello and walked straight in toward my room. I clearly couldn't talk to her about this new unexplained attraction I had for Arsen without her rude criticism. She didn't even respond when I spoke to her.

I laid back on my bed, wondering how I could possibly feel this way. This man had just threatened to take my life if I revealed his secret and I could feel nothing but lust for him after that. Was I going insane? In that brief moment of submission, I felt so alive. It was just something about the way he told me what to do and that look he gave me, like I had better listen to him or else. I wasn't sure why, but I thought I was letting my guard down. I thought I might be able to open up to someone new. Arsen was different from the rest and I thought it was time for me to actually deal with a real man.

I was definitely insane. I was risking my life, all for the sake of finding a lover who I could actually balance out with. I thought he could get over his hatred for me after seeing how trustworthy I would be with his secret. I turned on some music and started to sing along softly until I felt the presence of someone at my door.

"So you were just going to stay out all night with no call or text, then come home and not tell me where have you been?" Anabella asked from my doorway. I looked at her and shook my head.

"Ana, I called you like twenty times last night and you didn't answer the phone for me, which resulted in me staying the night at Arsen's house. I didn't think you would care to know where I've been since you ignored my phone calls and didn't even bother to respond when I just said hello to you." I rolled my eyes and continued to stare up at the ceiling.

"Did you call my new number? That would be the smart thing to do, Lola," she said. "And great. Just great. You're sleeping with this man now?"

"Since when do you have a new number and when were you going to tell me, Anabella?" I sat up quickly and looked directly at her. "I'm your best friend for Christ's sake. What if it was an emergency?! And how dare you? Nothing happened between Arsen and I!"

"I'm sure Arsen would be all the protection that you needed, Lola. And I definitely sent a text to all my contacts with my new number. You would have noticed if you had taken a break from that little novel of yours and paid attention to the real world." She scoffed. "Pathetic. I don't even know who you are anymore"

"Get out of my room, Anabella." I couldn't believe that my own best friend would even say such a thing like that to me.

She had been the only one who supported my decision to become a writer, but the last few days had been really tense between us. I wasn't sure where all of this built-up hate had come from inside of her, but I needed to find out, and I needed to know why she was directing it toward whatever Arsen and I have going on.

"Fine," she mumbled, folding her arms over her chest and leaving my bedroom.

I heard her say a few things under her breath, but I didn't care enough to extend the problem at hand. Since we were children, Anabella was always stubborn. She never cared if she was wrong or right as long as no one questioned her actions, and when her actions were questioned, she would catch an attitude. This specific problem never phased me because I was the most knowledgeable one in the friendship and she would always listen to me.

Since Arsen and I had begun talking, Anabella had taken her stubbornness to an entirely different level. She had been very moody and disapproving of everything that had been going on, although I was a grown woman who was completely capable of making her own conscious decisions. I wasn't quite sure what she didn't get about that.

Even if she didn't approve of who I was dating, she could at least support me being in a relationship—and that was the thing! Arsen and I weren't even dating, so I didn't see what the big deal was. Whatever we had between us could either go really badly or really well. All I knew was that I wished I could have my best friend there for me through it all.

I started to do a bit of studying to clear my mind, but also to gather some questions to ask Arsen. I searched his name on the internet and wrote down any interesting facts that caught my eye. I started downloading a couple of his books onto my laptop to read later. I wanted to know the ins and outs of his mind. One of his books caught my eye and I couldn't wait to read it.

The very first page caught my eye and I almost instantly fell in love with the story.

"Idyllic is what I would describe him as." I spoke into the phone, letting out a small laugh. I was in the community kitchen of my apartment, filling up a small bucket with ice. I heard my best friend mumble, slightly confused, on the other side of the phone.

"You barely even know the guy, Sarah. Plus, he's like ten times your ag." She sounded irritated. I could just imagine how hard she rolled her eyes, but something drew me to this guy—my new neighbor directly across the hall. We bumped into each other once in the hallway and the way he caught me was breathtaking. I don't know what it was.

Guys never really caught my eye, old or young. I was always on a level that they weren't. I liked to focus on my craft more than a silly relationship, but this was something different. His rich, tan skin and glistening smile. There was a little spark when I fell into his arms. The innocence of the touch drove me up the wall and I have yet to understand why.

"You don't get it, Rachel. I felt something." I smiled slightly and ran a finger around the rim of the silver bucket of ice.

"You're irritating, you know that?" she exclaimed with a very nasty tone of voice. I rolled my eyes and took a deep breath.

"Look, if you're going to continue with this lurid attitude, I don't think we should finish this phone call. Bye." And with that, I hung up the phone.

When she made it back to her room, she opened up her journal to the entry she wrote after meeting Arthur.

'He was just a guy and I was just a girl.

No, wait, he was more than that.

How could I devalue a soul with rich intellect and a consciousness that glows immensely to just a gender? Something so distant, something so man-made.

I want to know your thoughts. I want to feel your vibrations. I want our subconscious minds to linger around each other and engage in an experience our physical bodies can't.

I want to talk to you. I want to hear about your childhood, I want to know your deepest conspiracies, and I want you to take up all the space in my mind.

Feed me knowledge. Enlighten me.'

Sarah smiled down at the page before she started to draw hearts all over it. She felt that Arthur was the guy of her dreams.

The story of my life. Midway through reading, I found myself still thinking about the argument I had with Anabella again. So I decided to just let the situation go and get some rest before class and my meeting with Arsen tomorrow.

7

ARSEN

Why was Lola acting so ...seductive after I practically told her that I'd kill her? Why was she so eager to see me again after she found out about my drug cartel? This was all so strange. Did she really feel this way, or was this all apart of some type of scam from my enemy? I wasn't sure what it was, but I called a meeting with the guys at the clubhouse.

I picked up a pack of beer and brought it along with me to the meeting. The guys were very anxious to hear the news that I had for them. I didn't know how they'd react or what they'd say, but I just knew I had fucked up badly. Had I not taken the time to calm down, I would've never noticed that my hand was red and burning from how tightly I was gripping the steering wheel.

I just can't believe that something like that even happened. How could I be so stupid to have practically left all of my most important information out in the open? I just thought I'd be able to trust Lola enough to not do anything stupid like that, but boy was my judgment wrong. I started to think about how my entire empire could come crashing down if the world found out about this, and I became so angry that I just had to hurry inside before I lost my temper.

In the clubhouse, the guys and I gathered around the table. They all took seats while I stood before them. I put my hands behind my back and cleared my throat. I was afraid to tell them the news, but I knew that I had to be strong in front of them. My team would never do anything to me. I just had never told them news like this before so it was a new experience for me. This could also spark a new emotion that I had never seen in them.

How easy could it really be to break news like this to them? How could I tell them our future lives were in danger?

"All right, guys, here's the bad news." They all sighed and threw up their arms in anger. "I know. Bad news is a rare thing around here, but we are in serious trouble now."

"What kind of trouble, boss?" Pete, one of the members, asked.

"So, there's this girl who I met after doing a seminar at her school a couple of days ago and she's gorgeous. I mean, the most beautiful girl I have ever laid eyes on." I took a deep breath and continued. "To make a long story short, we went on a date and she came home with me. I let her stay in my home while I was at work today."

"Well why would you do that, boss?" David, another member, said.

"Don't ask. Anyway, I caught her going through my email and she found out about this drug cartel." I shook my head and took a deep breath waiting for their response.

All of the men gasped and looked around at each other. I could see the anger in their faces, but also the worry. A couple of men started discussing with each other what could go wrong if anyone else found out, and it felt like the weight of the world came crashing down on my shoulders. I knew that I had really messed up.

"What are we going to do about this? What are we going to do to the girl? No one can find out about this." Pete sounded confused, looking around at all of us.

"I say we kill the girl. If she isn't that popular around the school or if she's a nobody in general, there should be no problem if she dies. Right?" one of the other members spoke. The group waited in silence for my response

"Kill her?! I think we've killed enough people already," I said, covering the fact that I wanted to save her life because of the feelings I had towards her. "Plus, there's something really special about this girl."

"You like her or something?" Pete asked.

"That's beside the point here, Pete."

"I say you kidnap the girl. There's like a week left in school, right? Kidnap the girl and no one at the school will come looking for her because it's the summertime," David spoke up. "There's no point in killing the girl when you can use her to work for you"

I ran my index finger and thumb over my chin. "Hmm, sounds like a pretty cool idea."

All of the guys simultaneously agreed that that would be the best option and we began to plan it out. The guys and I came up with the best way possible to get Lola to fall for this trap. Tomorrow at our interview I would see if Lola would come over to my place for dinner after her last day of classes. Then I would explain to her that she was going to stay and work for me until everything was settled between us. Hopefully, some other things would happen between us, but I'd save that for later.

8

LOLA

I finally finished my math final and it was time for me to go to my interview with Arsen. I changed my outfit from a simple t-shirt and jeans to a form-fitting skirt with a button down, leaving the few top buttons loose to show off my cleavage. I put on a simple pair of heels and pulled my hair up into a tight bun. I went for my everyday makeup, which was natural but with a bold lip. I knew that Arsen would love what I was wearing, so that made me feel more confident than usual. I got in my car and headed over to his office.

Upon entering, I saw the same gorgeous girl at the front desk. For some reason, that made me really jealous and I began to wonder if Arsen had ever tried anything with her. I mean, she was flawless. She had great hair, a great body, and a nice smile ... but she wasn't me. I walked up to the front desk and flashed a fake smile.

"Lola Anderson for a scheduled meeting with Mr. Lockhart at three p.m." I stared at her as she clicked through the computer. She told me to just walk into his office and that he would be waiting for me. Perfect.

I walked towards his office, once again loving the sound of

my heels clicking against the ground. I made it to his door and knocked three times. I heard him mumble for me to come in, so I proceeded to enter. I watched and he looked up from his desk. He was wearing his reading glasses and had on a navy blue suit. I felt this tingly feeling in my stomach.

"Hello, Arsen." I smiled and took a seat in front of his desk. I pulled my notebook from my bag and opened it to where I had left off after our last meeting. "How are you today?"

"I'm fine, Lola. How are you?" I saw his eyes go from my eyes to my chest and back up to my face. He smirked and leaned back in his chair, holding the back of his pen between his teeth.

"I'm amazing." I let out a small laugh, "So, Mr. Lockhart, I did a little studying on your pieces of work and I wanted to talk a bit about your book, 'The Midnight Hour." It's more erotic than I expected, but it really caught my eye."

"Yes. That's one of my favorite books that I've written." He folded his hands together and placed them on his lap. "What about it sparked your interest?"

"The age difference." I smiled and he raised an eyebrow. "Also, the way you write. I love how the story alternates between both of the character's point of view. You have a way with words that really capture the reader's eye, Mr. Lockhart."

"Thank you, Lola." He smiled. Just then, there was a knock, and a pretty woman stuck her head through the door.

"Sorry to interrupt, Mr. Lockhart. I have your coffee." She walked in wearing an outfit similar to mine. She placed his coffee on the desk and flashed a sly smile. "Have a nice day, Mr. Lockhart."

Arsen smirked and watched her as she left. I raised an eyebrow in slight jealousy and cleared my throat. "Um. I should make myself a bit more comfortable."

I pulled my hair from its bun and let it fall over my shoulders. Arsen's eyes widened at the sight, and I knew I had him back in the position I wanted him.

"Now." I smiled. "What inspired you to write 'The Midnight Hour?'"

"My attraction to women like you inspired me, Lola." He chuckled. "My dominant traits inspired that book as well."

"My attraction to men like you makes me want to read your story a million times." I laughed and began writing in my notes. "Tell me about your favorite book, Arsen."

"Well, for starters, I'll tell you the name of the book. It's 'Can't Buy Love,' by Nicholas Hunter." he spoke and I jotted this down as fast as I could before he could continue to explain what it was about. "It was the very first book I bought from the school store of the college I went to. I'd heard a slight buzz about it around town and decided to check it out."

I smiled softly and sat back in my seat, waiting for him to go further in detail.

"It was about a boy who had always dreamed of having as much money as he needed to buy whatever he wanted and he achieved that goal. But here's the twist—by having so much money, he attracted all of the wrong types of people to have friendships or relationships with. He learned that money can't buy love, and though it can buy you materialistic things, it can't bring you deep-rooted and eternal happiness." He smiled and watched as I copied that down into my notes.

"That's really beautiful. I'll definitely have to check that out."

"I have a copy that I could lend you one day," he offered.

"Wow, that'd be amazing. Thanks, Arsen." I blushed slightly.

He checked his watch and looked at me. "Well, Lola, I'm sorry to cut this short, but I have a meeting to attend." He sat up and took a sip of his coffee.

"Oh ...all right," I said, making the disappointment in my

voice clear. I began putting my notebook in my bag and rolled my eyes at how awkwardly short that was.

Arsen stood from his seat and grabbed my hand as he walked from around his desk to walk me to the door. "Now listen." He backed me into the door.

I began breathing heavily from how close he was. I stared into his eyes and he smiled.

"I have a very busy schedule this week. So I don't need you popping up with any interviews anytime soon. All right?" He grabbed my arms and slid his hands down to my waist. "Next Friday, after classes, get real pretty for me, all right? And meet me at the coffee shop at seven p.m. sharp. We're having dinner at my place."

I nodded slowly, not breaking contact. I felt his lips press against mine roughly and my knees buckled. I never expected for him to kiss me. One of his hands left my waist and held the back of my head, pulling me closer to him. There was absolutely no space between us and I felt my heart drop when he bit and tugged on my bottom lip.

"Now go." He pulled away, laughing, and used his thumb to wipe away any lipstick that he had smeared.

I licked my lips and just stared at him, not knowing what to say. That was the most breathtaking kiss I'd ever had, and the way he had taken it by force was the icing on the cake. He held the door open for me and I quickly fixed my hair before leaving. For the second time with Arsen, I felt nineteen again.

I walked away feeling like someone powerful. I felt like a new person ...like I had a life again. With being the uptight, all-work-no-play type of girl, life could get pretty hard. I was always stressing about what I had to do or what deadline I had to meet, but I didn't feel that way around Arsen. I thought that I might be letting my guard down a little too fast, but honestly, it was the best decision I'd made in a long time. This new rush of excitement completely took over me and I didn't think I could turn back. It was far too late now.

Being around Arsen made me feel like it was okay to take a break every once in a while and have fun, but to also go back and finish my craft later. But it had only been a few days, so I needed to slow down and really pay attention to who I was falling for. This man was a murderer—a new leader of the drug cartel! What had I gotten myself into?

9

ARSEN

I knew she wanted that kiss as badly as I did, and I knew that the kiss would definitely leave her wanting more. I didn't really have a meeting. I just wanted to leave her on edge. I knew that even the strongest, most independent girl couldn't hold herself back. I knew my magic, and it only took a couple of days. I chuckled to myself and walked back to my desk, taking a sip of my coffee while looking out the view of the window. I had everything I wanted in the palm of my hand.

Lola made me feel young again. Being around her took me back to when I was around her age and just starting to discover what love was all about. That was a time when I was wild and adventurous. I had a lot of down time and could really be myself without any consequences. That's why being with her was such a valuable time for me.

I felt as if she was really the one for me and that was why it hurt me so much that she would betray me. I thought that if her feelings were almost the same as mine, she would at least respect my privacy. Whether my email was left open or not, it wasn't her place to take a look inside.

That whole situation angered me so much, but I just couldn't force myself to be over-the-top upset with her. I knew that showing extreme anger toward her would make me uncomfortable and I couldn't bring myself to hurt her ...that much.

My phone began to ring,

disrupting my thoughts and making me slightly irritated. It was a call from David. I answered quickly because it was rare for David to call me in the middle of the day.

"Boss, you're not going to like this." His voice sounded frantic and I almost didn't want to hear what he was going to say.

"What is it?" I kept my calm. Panicking just as much as him was going to help nothing at that moment.

"That lady who has been chasing you down for years says she's coming after the girl and it's not going to be pretty."

"The girl ...what girl?" I asked in confusion.

"The one you went out with the other night, you know? The one who found out about us," he said. There was a silence on the phone after that as I took a minute to think.

"How'd you figure that out?" I asked.

"She sent me an email from her husband's account that he had with us and said these words exactly."

Dear David and crew,

Since Arsen stole the love of my life from me, I guess I'll have to take something from his as well. That girl—his new arm candy. My daughter has been telling me she's seen them around town together and it's more than just taking her out to make himself look good. He has feelings for this girl and this is the perfect time for me to come in and make my move. I just hope you guys get a hold of her before I do.

"It's crazy, boss," David spoke. "This woman is absolutely out of her mind."

"Oh, this isn't good ...this is not good, David." I found myself panicking just as much as David. It was bad enough that all of the guys hated her. Now this random lady was after her because she saw us at dinner one night together. Who was her daughter and why was she watching our every move?

"What, do you love this chick or something?" David asked in an almost disgusted tone.

"Just find out where that lady is and handle her," I spat and hung up the phone.

Love? Pssh, whatever. Sure, I was fond of her, but I was most certain I didn't love someone I barely knew. My jaw clenched and I stormed out of my office. Maybe I did love her ...but how? I've barely known her for that long. How could these feelings for her be so strong?

I decided I was going to go home early. After taking my keys from the assistant, I made my way out to my car. Hopefully the ride back to my place would calm me down. I turned on some soothing music and took in the beauty of the city.

I inhaled the fresh air that blew through the window as I drove up the driveway of my home. When I made it inside, I completely ignored the workers there for the weekly cleaning and went straight to my bedroom. I took off my shirt and tossed myself back onto the bed, feeling more comfort than I expected.

I began to think about Lola and how much her personality reminded me of my ex-wife. Yes, the shy and innocent girls were fun to toy around with every now and then, but the open and hardworking ones were the type of girls I'd considered actually being with.

My ex-wife was a lawyer, and very loud and opinionated. We met at a convention for young innovators when we were in our early twenties and fell in love. We had an unbreakable bond up until a couple of years after our first daughter was born. She became a different person, and I knew that being a mother and raising a child could change you in some ways, but she didn't even try to do anything the same anymore. She completely shut me out when we were supposed to be a family. Where she crossed the line is when she cheated on me.

It would have made sense for me to be the one who cheated, since women had been throwing themselves at me since my ex-wife and I met, but, no. She fell in love with someone new, and in the back of my mind I always beat myself up about that. I wondered what he did for her that I hadn't, or what I had done wrong in general. Everyone told me that it was all her, but I just felt that I had some responsibility with that.

Being around Lola brought back those feelings that I had with my ex-wife, and that's another reason why I couldn't bear to be around her for so long. I didn't want to fall for the wrong person, thinking that I could get back what I used to have. I guessed that kidnapping her next Friday would actually help me find out if she was the one or not.

"Hey, boss. I just got a call and you're not going to like this," one of the members in the back spoke up.

"What's up?" I asked, not really ready to hear what other bad news had to be stacked on top of the situation at hand.

"Ronnie, down at the harbor, says the new guy got away with a couple of boxes of the drugs. He says he didn't notice a few of the boxes missing until the car was speeding off and he saw them in the back seat."

"What fucking new guy?! I didn't hire anyone new! It should only be the five men that I sent down there originally." I slammed my hands on the desk. "We let some random get away with a few boxes of our product?"

I couldn't believe this was happening. First, my life's in danger because an outside knows my illegal source of income and now a large amount of my product has been stolen. I picked up a bottle of beer and launched it across the room. It shattered as it hit the wall and beer went everywhere.

"Clean this fucking mess up," I spat. "And come up with how we'll find this son of a bitch by morning or things aren't going to be pretty."

10

LOLA

Great! An entire week without Arsen after he kissed me like that. I laid in my bed, staring up at the ceiling. I had no classes or finals to take that day, so I had nothing better to do. I sat up, grabbed my laptop from my bedside table, and opened it quickly. I thought, what better to do right than continue to read where I left off from Arsen's book, 'The Midnight Hour.'

I began reading from page thirty-six. The main character, Arthur, had just awakened from a long, steamy night with his lover. It was like Arsen described his character's feelings almost as if they were his own.

Have you ever looked at someone? Like really looked at them. Did you take a minute to admire the beauty that lays upon them?

I have. I do it every day.

Looking at Sarah is a pleasant moment I experience every day. Taking even the slightest second of the day to admire her inspires me so much. She's so deep-rooted into my poetry that I could write about my love for anything in the world and still find a way to reference my feelings for her.

She and I are meant for each other. I know this because our souls vibrate on a higher level together. Without her, I would probably be an old man down in the dumps every day because I haven't found my true love.

My favorite part of the day is watching her. She's my favorite movie. I like the way she lotions her legs, mimicking rich and fancy women. I love the way she laughs at the littlest things I do. I love the crinkle in her nose when she giggles, and most of all I love the way she loves me.

Despite the age difference, she and I truly love each other. And, no, we aren't accepted in society, but we are going to continue to let our love grow strong. We're both grown and consenting adults and we should be able to love each other without any judgment. Sadly, this isn't how the world works.

Fuck what the world thinks. I am in love with Sarah Hughes and nothing's going to change that. The way she moves when she dances, the look on her face when I tell her she's beautiful, and how she's so carefree with whatever she's doing. And that's why I'm writing this right now, because the feelings I have for her are too strong for just a short, simple poem.

She changed my life so much that there has to be another way to show that I really care for her. I love her and I'll love her until the day that I die.

I sighed and smiled to myself. What if Arsen thinks of me the same way Arthur thinks of Sarah. I must've said that aloud, because Anabella let out a loud laugh as walked past my room.

"Yeah, right." She snickered as she walked down the hall.

I quickly stood from my bed, tired of her attitude, and walked down the hall into her room where she'd just entered.

"And what exactly is your problem, Ana? You've had an attitude since I met Arsen. Why can't you just be happy that I actually like someone?"

She turned her back to me and sat on her bed. "You dumb, silly, little girl. You're sleeping with the enemy."

"The enemy?! What are you even talking about, Anabella?" I asked, genuinely confused about what exactly she meant by Arsen being the enemy. "And I'm not sleeping with Arsen. Let's make that clear."

"Wow," she scoffed. "Some best friend you are."

"What, are you jealous?"

"Of what?" she laughed harshly.

"The fact that I'm out having fun without you? Or maybe even the fact that you can't hold on to a man, but now that I have one it's rubbing you the wrong way? Is that it?!"

"You're trash, Lola! How could you say that to me? Are you really going to let some random man come between us?" she screamed. We were now standing face to face and she was on a verge of tears.

"I should ask you the same thing, since you've been acting as if I'm nothing to you since Arsen and I met!!"

"If you don't remember one of the biggest things I've ever told you, things would be better off if we didn't talk anymore."

"But Ana! I'm so confused. What are you talking—"

"Just go, Lola!!" She cut me off and I threw my hands up in defeat.

"Whatever, Anabella. I guess I'll see you around." I had no choice but to go back to my room, disappointed and confused. There I was trying to resolve the issues between us and she couldn't even tell me what was going on so I could fix it. Why did she believe Arsen was 'the enemy' and what was the big thing that she mentioned?

A couple of days passed slowly but surely. Class after class, final after final, and I had to do it all on my own, without Anabella there to tell me that I'd do fine or to let me know that she'd be there for me. I felt empty. I tried making small talk with the other students and even the professors, but it just didn't feel right. I hadn't been alone like that in a long time.

On the bright side, I had been working on my novel. It's based on a teenage girl who has not a care in the world. She goes by herself on an adventure through different states and learns a lot of life lessons along the way. Being who she is, the trip through various cities and areas full of nature help heal her. It gives her closure from past struggles and a sense of relief from the issues she faces in the present, making her outlook for the future positive.

There was a spin on the story, though, to keep it interesting. The reason this girl went on an 'adventure' was to escape from the weird guy who had been stalking her for months. I finished up the remainder of the draft for my story intro.

"It's like boys are manifested with trouble," I sighed as I laid back onto my bed. I could feel the cool breeze from the air vents cause goosebumps to swell all over my arms and legs. My silk gown wasn't doing much to cover my body.

"Oh, girl, I'm sure it's just someone playing a joke on you," Shandy said, smiling.

"No! This is serious, Shandy!" I half-yelled angrily. "Do you know what it's like to be stalked? I'm always being watched. It's scary and it's getting in the way of my job, new relationships, and just everything in general!!"

Shandy bit the inside of her cheek gently and her eyes widened slightly. "What are we going to do about this?"

"I don't know." I closed my eyes tightly and took a deep breath. "I really don't know. I just need to get away."

It's all a big representation of who I am, who I used to be, and who I'm becoming. It's my life experience dramatized through a life I wish I lived—a life that I will live after my dreams of becoming a best-selling author comes true. The way that Arsen's favorite book made him feel was exactly how my own novel made me feel. As though, even if the character was fictional, there was still someone out there who I could connect to. I was often guilty of getting lost in my own writings.

I would usually have had Anabella critique my writing, but after the situation between us, it was like living with a stranger. We didn't acknowledge each other anymore. The worst part about it all was that I was starting to see her hang out with a new group of friends. I just wanted to know where we went wrong.

I let my English professor look over my work instead. She gave me a couple pointers on how to go about writing certain things and just scanned through a few of the pages that I had already written, but overall, she said it was a pretty cool story. The words 'pretty cool' made me uncomfortable. I didn't want my story to be seen as 'pretty cool,' but rather spontaneous, refreshing, or life changing.

Random thoughts of how my work could possibly not make it far in the writing business flooded my head. I knew that I was a great writer, but the weight of everything happening plus the "compliment" I had just received from my teacher made me think otherwise. I knew there had to be a way to get myself back on track.

I shook the negative thoughts from my head and started to walk back to my room from class. As I approached the building, I spotted the lady who had attacked Arsen at the restaurant. She was leaving the building that I lived in and seeing her in broad daylight, she looked strangely familiar. I walked with my head down until she was out of sight so she wouldn't see me and assumed it had something to do with Arsen murdering her husband.

I started to think about how messed up that situation actually was and I felt horrible. I couldn't imagine that happening to me or my family, if I had one. I finally made it past her without her noticing and caught the elevator up to my room. When I made it inside of my suite, there were about four or five other people sitting on the couch watching TV. Ana was sitting in the middle of them.

Seeing her doing something that we always did together with some random people made me feel less important—like this entire relationship actually ended over something that I wasn't completely aware of. I stormed into my room and lay out on my bed, burying my face into the pillow. I let out a muffled scream of frustration, then sat up straight. I just wanted everything to be back to normal.

It had officially been an entire week since the kiss with Arsen and the argument with Anabella, and I hadn't talked to either of them since. I didn't talk to many other people on campus, so when it came time for me to rant about anything, I could only talk to myself. It felt like I was going crazy. It was definitely not fun being the only person I could talk to.

I had just finished my last final of the school year and decided to get a cup of coffee to wake myself up. Everyone must have really been in a hurry to get home because the line for coffee wasn't as long or as slow as usual. The campus was almost empty. It was finally summer.

I got a cup of coffee and a danish. This was the only thing that had been able to put a real smile on my face for the last couple of days.

The walk to and from the coffee shop, and the actual coffee itself, was what I needed to clear my mind from everything that had been going on lately. Though I felt pretty bored and alone, these were the moments that I needed to keep myself sane. It was always good to take the time to reassure yourself that everything was going to be all right and that you could always move forward in any problem as long as you worked hard enough.

I took a seat on a bench next to a girl with sandy brown hair. I wanted to see if my attempt to make small talk would work because, quite frankly, I was tired of talking to myself.

"Hi." I looked over at her. "I'm Lola. What's your name?"

"Daisy." She smiled and looked over at me. "I know who you are, Lola. I've always wanted to hang out with you." She laughed nervously.

"Why didn't you say anything?" She just looked at me and I caught on. "Let me guess. The email that I sent to the entire school claiming I didn't need distractions from my work?"

"You're right," she laughed. "What made you want to talk to me?"

"Just decided to be social for once." I smiled slightly. "I thought it'd be cool to actually have fun once in a while."

"I understand," she spoke.

"So, do you have any plans for the summer?" I asked.

"Well, yeah. There are tons of flyers going around for some upcoming parties and bonfires." She began pulling out pieces of folded paper from her bag. "You can have these. I already have the information on my phone.

"Thanks, Daisy!" I smiled big and put the flyers inside of my bag.

"A couple of friends and I are hosting a big 'end of the semester' party event tomorrow. You should come out." She mimicked my smile.

"I'll definitely keep that in mind." I stood up and waved. "See you around!"

Did I just make a friend? The end of my junior year of college and I was finally making a friend other than Anabella. Why did this feel so great? Was it because I had found someone who could fill this empty part of me or because I just missed the feeling of having multiple friends when I was younger? Who knows. I was just glad that I didn't have to be alone anymore.

As soon as I got back into my room, my phone rang. It was Arsen. After this long period of not speaking, I thought I would be the one to call first. I answered and put the phone up to my ear slowly.

"Come over tonight." Those were the only words that he spoke. His voice was deeper and darker than usual. It sent chills up my spine.

"What time? I thought I was meeting you at the coffee shop."

"You know what ...just come over now."

"I—is there anything that you need in particular, Arsen?"

"Stop talking and come over now," he demanded. I'd never been more attracted to him than I was that very moment. He hung up the phone and I sat there speechless. I decided to slip into something more appealing. I took a quick shower and threw on a dress similar to the one I wore when we first went out, with fishnets and a pair of nude heels. Little did anyone know, I was hiding a beautiful set of red lace lingerie underneath. I put loose curls in my hair and wore no makeup, except for my favorite burgundy lipstick and a little mascara. I was sure I knew what he wanted, but if things went a different way I wasn't so sure how I'd feel.

The drive to his house felt like I was on top of the world. I was in my own car, blasting my favorite music, with the wind blowing in my hair. Once again, I was feeling like the nineteen-year-old me. I had a feeling that my life was about to take a turn that I never expected. This could be the start of something new.

I pulled up to his house and parked off to the side. A couple of seconds after ringing the doorbell, I was greeted by the nice lady who helped me last time.

"Well, hello, beautiful. It's a pleasure to see you back here."

She smiled and stood off to the side so that I could go in. "Mr. Lockhart is waiting for you in the master bedroom."

I thanked her and took my time walking up the stairs. With every step I took toward that room, I felt the anticipation rise. I knew that there was going to be something interesting behind those doors, but I couldn't imagine what it could be. I got closer to the door and placed my hand on the doorknob.

11

ARSEN

As soon as I heard her hand on the other side of the door, I knew it was 'go time.' I quickly opened the door and she jumped slightly. I grabbed her wrist, pulling her inside, shutting the door behind us, and pressing her up against it. She groaned quietly and I placed a few kisses on her neck. I felt her body become tense, so it was time for me to lay out some ground rules.

"Now you listen to me, and you listen closely." I spoke in a stern voice, asserting my dominance.

Her eyes widened as she nodded slowly. "O—Okay."

"Nah-uh." I pulled her hands over her head and gripped both of her wrists with one of my hands. "From now on, you answer with 'yes sir.' Do I make myself clear?"

"Yes sir." She bit down on her lip and I smirked. I loved seeing her under my control. I wanted her to submit to me. I wanted to have complete dominance over her.

"Whatever I say, you do." I chuckled. "You didn't really think that tough girl act was going to cut it around me, did you?"

She opened her mouth to speak, but I cut her off. "Think before you answer, Lola."

"No, sir," she said quietly.

"Louder, Lola." I pushed myself closer to her.

"No, sir!!" she squealed and I felt the pace of her breathing increase.

"That's a really beautiful dress you're wearing, Lola." I spoke in a low tone, but loud enough for her to hear me. "Take it off."

I let go of her wrists and took a step back so that she could get undressed. She turned her back to me and slowly let down the zipper of her dress. She let the straps fall down her arms slowly and proceeded to pull it off of her chest. From where I was standing, it looked like a simple red bra, but then she turned around and the lace took me by surprise. I could see her beautiful breast through the thin material she had on.

She slid the rest of her dress down to her ankles and kicked it across the room. She had on a matching pair of lace panties underneath her fishnet stockings. They looked so beautiful laid across her long legs. I sat on the bed and just admired her beauty. Everything was happening in my favor and I couldn't be happier.

"Take off the stockings and bring them to me. When you make it over here, lay across my lap and do not make a sound."

And that's just what she did. Without hesitation, she complied with each demand, and I loved every moment of it.

When she made it over to the bed she stood in front of me. She placed the stockings in my hand and laid across my lap. Laughing slightly under my breath, I pulled both of her hands behind her back and tied them together,

"Good girl," I said, and she moaned slightly under her breath. I gave her a spank right on her ass and she squirmed in discomfort. "I thought I told you specifically to not make a sound, Lola. Don't make me punish you."

"Yes, sir," she whined, and I gave her another spank.

"Don't say another word," I instructed. I lifted her body and tossed her on the bed. I brushed her hair back out of her face to admire her beauty. Her skin was perfect and the color of lipstick she had chosen really made her eyes glow. I looked her directly in the eyes and said, "You're never going home."

Her face went from seductive to panicked. It made me chuckle to see how frightened she'd gotten. She was about to open her mouth, but I warned her that, if she screamed, although no one would hear her, she'd be in serious trouble.

12

LOLA

"You're never going home." Arsen spoke as he looked me directly in the eyes. It was like the words rolled off his tongue as slowly as possible.

Just when I thought life was going great, everything went to shambles. I watched as he laughed right in my face, as if I was nothing. *Maybe this was all a part of the roleplay*, I thought to myself, but there I went again, making up silly excuses in my head to make light of the situation. I guess it was a way to make myself calm and comfortable.

I thought back to Anabella calling me a dumb, stupid, little girl. That's exactly how I felt right now, because that's exactly what I was for trusting a man who I barely knew. There was just something about Arsen's aura that just pulled me in. His charm and witty sense of humor really captured my heart. Even with everything going on, I could feel myself falling harder for him.

I somewhat understand why he would keep me here 'forever.' I knew his biggest secret and he didn't want anyone to find out. He was just protecting himself—maybe even the both of us. Maybe someone else found out that I knew the secret and was out to get me and this was Arsen's way of protecting me? Why else would he wait an entire week to do something about the situation?

Whether he was doing this for us or just himself, I still felt stupid for the way I caved. I submitted to him so easily that it was embarrassing. I had never been so obedient and controlled in my entire life, not even as a child. My parents were never really the most chill parents in the world, but they definitely were not as demanding as Arsen.

I felt my panties become wet at just the thought of Arsen having full dominance over what I did and said. I wished he would come back to finish what he had started, but I knew that wasn't going to happen. So I sat there, close to tears, and not knowing how feel or what to do next.

I felt hopeless at this point. My arms were tied up, so if I'd tried to make any escape, it would be ten times harder than it should. I shifted onto my side and laid down. It was a little uncomfortable for a while, but soon my body became numb and I couldn't feel a thing.

So many thoughts were flying through my brain that I couldn't even decide what to think about first. I eventually got so confused about everything that was going off that I just let myself fall asleep to take a temporary break from all of the madness.

13

ARSEN

I left her sitting on the bed and went to my office to check a few emails and see if there was any new information from the guys. I was scrolling through a load of emails from people contacting me to do events and lectures around the world. The guys sent a few messages about how they found out the woman's name and address. Now they were coming up with a plan of how to get rid of her. I sent out a few replies and continued to scroll through pointless messages until one message in particular caught my eye.

It was titled 'Watch your back, Arsen," and it read:

Dear Arsen Lockhart,

I know what you're up to. As if you didn't think murdering my father was enough, now you're fooling around with my best friend?

I raised an eyebrow. What was this person talking about?

The fact that she actually gives you the time of day makes me wonder if is she that stupid or if you are just really good at playing these games. My father has been dead for a year now and if you think my mom and I have forgotten, you have another thing coming. Enjoy your peaceful life as much as you can, Arsen.

The letter wasn't signed with any name, but when I thought

about it, the girl who sat next to Lola the same day that I gave that seminar looked a lot like the woman at the restaurant. That woman had said her daughter had been watching Lola and me around town, and the only person who could possibly know who we both were and what has been going on between us was Lola's best friend. Was it possible that I had killed Lola's best friend's father?

A BILLIONAIRE'S TROUBLES

An Alpha Billionaire Romance

By Michelle Love

14

ARSEN

During the entire process of abducting Lola and holding her hostage, I could do nothing but keep her comfort first in my mind. The boys had wanted to keep her inside of some rough, cold building where she had very little water and food, but I couldn't bring myself to do that to her. I couldn't have lived with myself if I had done that to her. With anyone else, I would've done it in a heartbeat and maybe even have taken their life without any thought put into it. With Lola, things were just different. They had to be different because something about her led me to believe that she was the one I'd been searching for years after my divorce.

I wanted to deny my strong attraction to her, but every time I did, my feelings just became stronger. I even had to take a deep breath before walking into her room. She doesn't know that she's my weakness. She's not even a little aware of how hard I've tried to remain calm around her.

I went into her room, admiring her beauty from behind. I called her name and watched her jump. I hope I sent shivers down her spine. I had to brace myself for when she turned around. When I saw her face, I had to hold back a smile. She looked very well rested and sort of happy, but when her eyes met mine, her face cringed into a look of disgust. She was definitely upset with me.

I gave her the two spiral notebooks and pens I had for her. One of the books I gave her to write in when she was bored and the other was a list of things I needed her to do for me. I didn't know if she noticed when she flipped through a couple of pages, but a couple of those tasks involved spending time with me for a couple of days—dinner dates, some trips to the mall, and outings to a couple of other places. Hopefully, those outings could lead to us having mutual feelings for each other, because at this moment it seemed like I had more feelings for her than she had for me.

Kissing her was a part of my plan. I wanted her to feel the feelings I had for her, because clearly being nice after kidnapping her wouldn't work. As much as I wanted to take her right there on that bed, I couldn't. I had to resist as much as possible.

I'd be lying if I said the thought of her curvy body wasn't always in the back of my mind. It was. Each and every day, I imagined my hands moving up and down her smooth waist and pulling her body close to mine. I longed for her touch. It killed me inside that I couldn't have her the way I wanted. Why did she have to fuck up?

I shook my head angrily at the thought and continued on with my day. There was a meeting today with the guys and me. We were getting together to talk about what was new with the whole kidnapping situation and what was new with the cartel in general. This cartel was first put together by David and me, around the time we both became very money hungry. We were looking for ways to make more money, and David, being my best friend since childhood, was doing nothing but looking out for me when he suggested this idea. A drug cartel full of millionaires. Yes, I said it. A drug cartel full of millionaires.

Each and every one of us had worked our way up to an outstanding amount of money coming in daily because of our jobs and also this cartel. If anyone found out about this, we wouldn't lose much money because we already had a lot saved up, but we could ruin our reputations within our careers. Not to mention, we could do a lot of time in jail. That was why the boys were so anxious to get rid of Lola, but I really didn't think that she would be the one to take down our entire cartel.

If she really wanted to sabotage us, she would have acted quickly. There were no messages or emails on her phone and laptop about the situation, so I doubt that she even had a plan to expose us in the first place. The guys made it seem as if she was working with the enemy and they knew the easiest way to get inside of my house was by using a young, pretty girl.

That logic didn't make sense, simply because of the fact that Lola was playing extremely hard to get. If the enemy sent her over to get any information from me, then I would have had sex with her the first day we met. She wouldn't have hesitated to spend the night at my place either. The guys really kept coming up with these outrageous theories about her, but she was just a normal girl who got caught being very nosey.

"Hey, what's up guys?!" I greeted the guys as I walked into our clubhouse. Similarly to the meeting from last week, the guys sat in a group behind the table and I stood in front of it. They greeted me back with various 'hey's' and 'what's up's.'

"So, what's up with the chick, boss?" David sat up in his chair.

"Yeah, boss. Did you get the job done?" Pete spoke.

"What do you mean did I get the job done?" I cocked an eyebrow and crossed my arms over my chest, waiting for a response. "There was never a job to begin with."

"Did you kill the girl?!" one of the other members yelled.

"No, I didn't kill her," I spoke.

"She knows too much, boss," Pete added.

"Look! I told you idiots that she only knows that the drug cartel exists and that I killed that woman's husband. That's it. She literally knows nothing else," I spat angrily. How dare they question me about killing her when that was never the plan in the first place.

Silence filled the void air between us as the guys looked at me, taken aback by my reaction. I paced back and forth for a few seconds to blow off some steam. I couldn't handle the thought of Lola actually being dead, especially because of me.

"What's the update on the missing packages?" I sighed and took a seat. Someone handed me a beer and I took a quick swig.

"We have the names and location. We were going to send a few of our best men out to get them tonight." Pete took a swig of his beer and looked directly at me.

I nodded. "Let's get their things ready."

"Yes, sir," they all said in unison, with the exception of David. I could tell by the look on his face that he was thinking really hard about something. He wasn't paying much attention to anything that was going on around him.

"You two," I pointed to the two guys in the back. "Get the bags, and the rest of you get the guns ready"

I sat back in my chair and watched as everyone left the room. Again, all but David. I grabbed a cigar from the box on the table and lit it.

"You really like this girl, huh?" David chuckled, looking up at me.

"I do." I took a drag from the cigar and blew out the smoke in his direction. I kept a straight face. "Why are you asking me this?"

"Why else would you spare her life, Arsen?"

"She's the one, David. I'm so serious when I say this." I took a deep breath and brushed my hair back with my free hand.

"How are you so sure?" His eyebrows knitted together in confusion. "She's a little college girl."

"No, David. She's a grown woman, and I know she's the one because Lola makes me feel the same way she did. Maybe even a little better."

"Damn," he laughed slightly. "You really are feeling this girl. Now I know why you lashed out. I'm surprised that you even went through with the kidnapping plan if your feelings for her are that strong."

"That's the thing, man. I'm torn between loving her and killing her." I shook my head. "I don't think I could bring myself to do it, but the thought seems tempting. I couldn't live with her being dead, but I could definitely live without the fear of falling madly in love again. You get what I'm saying?"

"I understand man." He sighed. "It's just going to take time, all right? Don't stress yourself out."

I flashed the slight smile and put out my cigar. What I really needed right now was some rest. I hadn't slept much for the past few days, so I was just running off of multiple cups of coffee. I said my goodbyes to David, telling him to pass the message along to the rest of the team, and left.

The drive back home was shorter than I expected and I was thankful for that. Immediately after making it inside of the house, I quickly walked to my room. I wasted no time taking off my clothes and hopping into the shower. The warm water kissed my skin and I swear it felt like heaven on Earth. I found myself humming along to the song that was playing softly when I entered Lola's room earlier. It made me think of how beautiful the shower would have been if I were to share it with her.

My mind started to fill up with the thought of her. Whenever I tried to think of something different, it just brought me back to her. She reminded me of the sunset. How it's so warm but so vibrant, and it could make your whole day better just by looking at it. She was like caffeine in the morning. As much as you had been warned to stay away from it, it was addicting and you needed it to get through the day. She stood tall like a sunflower, beautiful and bright. The perfect combination.

Who would have suspected that I, Arsen Lockhart, would ever find love again? Now, I just had to figure out if she loved me back.

15

LOLA

I woke up in a room I'd never seen before. I looked to the left and the view was almost the same as the view from Arsen's house. I looked down and I wasn't tied up anymore, nor was I wearing the same outfit from the night before. I was dressed in a satin top with matching shorts. I pulled myself out of bed and walked to the door. When I tried opening it, it was locked. No matter how hard I pushed or pulled it wouldn't open.

With a sigh, I turned and went to look at myself in the mirror. My hair looked freshly brushed, which was odd. I pulled it into a ponytail with the hair tie that was on my wrist. I looked down and saw a note laying on the dresser. It had my name on it. I was a bit hesitant about picking it up, but maybe it would explain why the door was locked.

After a couple of seconds of deciding, I finally opened the letter. It explained that there were two doors inside of the room. One led to a walk-in closet, while the other led to a bathroom. It said that there would be various pieces of clothing that were my size inside of the closet. I read over a few more lines about where certain things were in the room and I finally made it to the end, which was what I was looking for.

The reason the door was locked, according to the note, was because I didn't deserve as much freedom as I wanted. The note was clearly written by Arsen, because it said that I should think about the consequences of my absurd actions. He wrote that he had had a hard time deciding if I should work for him until he trusted me again or if he should kill me. He also mentioned that my phone had been taken away and any source of connecting with someone outside of the house had been blocked off of the computer in the room and my laptop, which he had found in my car.

I rolled my eyes and crumbled the note into a ball. I couldn't believe that this was happening to me all because I looked through a couple of emails. What I really wanted to know was why it had taken him so long to take action against me. What about the situation changed his mind? Did someone else know?

That's it. Maybe he told the members of his cartel and they put this entire plan together. That had to have happened, because what else would've made Arsen change his mind so suddenly?

I shook my head and slid my feet as I walked back over to the bed. I plopped down and buried my face in the pillow. I let out a muffled scream to release the built-up anger in me. There was a knock on a door, followed by the voice of the woman I had met the first time I was there.

"Ms. Lola, your breakfast is ready," she spoke.

I got up quickly when I heard the door unlock from the outside. It pushed open slowly and she came inside, walking toward me with a tray of food. It smelled so delicious. I couldn't wait to eat. As she sat the tray down on the bed, I eyed the cracked door, thinking about whether I'd be able to make it out to find my car keys.

I guess she noticed, because she grabbed both of my arms and looked into my eyes.

"Don't even try it," she whispered. "There are two big guards out there."

I nodded slowly. "Do you know when I'll be getting out?"

"No." She shook her head. "Mr. Lockhart doesn't tell me much"

"Two questions." I looked at her and she nodded, agreeing to answer them. "What's your name? And why are you always so nice to me?"

"I'm Ms. Rose, the maid." She smiled. "You remind me so much of myself when I was younger—independent and spending time with older men. Seeing you makes me nostalgic. After over-hearing Arsen explain the situation between you two, I thought you could use all of the support I can give right now"

"Thank you so much." I smiled and hugged her. She jumped, not expecting the hug but returning the gesture. She reminded me a lot of my grandmother, who I was really looking forward to seeing this summer, but that plan was ruined because of Arsen.

"Rose, what is taking you so long?" One of the guards asked in a menacing tone.

"I gave you extra bacon." She smiled and left the room swiftly, closing and locking it behind her. I smiled softly to myself, knowing that someone cared, and crawled back into bed. On the tray were waffles, bacon, eggs, and a bowl of fruit. I was also given a cup of tea with a little bowl of sugar on the side.

After I finished eating, I decided to take a shower. The bathroom looked exactly like Arsen's, so I knew how everything worked. I walked back into the room and went on the computer to play some music. To my surprise, Arsen had a lot of the music I listened to on there already. I made a quick playlist and turned the volume all the way up so that I could hear it in the bathroom.

I started my shower and actually enjoyed my time in there. Some of my favorite songs were playing and I was using all of these fancy and expensive skin and hair care products. I didn't know if Arsen intended for that to happen, but I was actually starting to have a good day.

I got out of the shower and wrapped a towel around my body. I didn't want to put on the same clothes, so I went into the closet to see what was there for me. Upon entering, I expected to see just a small amount of clothing, but this was more than that. What was before my eyes was an entirely new wardrobe. There were all types of outfits. There were everyday outfits, night out outfits, an array of night clothing, and even all types of shoes. I looked into the drawers of the dresser and saw different types of undergarments and lingerie. I started looking at the tags and everything was the right size. Just like the note had said.

This was sort of strange, but I guessed it would come in handy during my time there. But if I was going to be held in this room for the time being, why would I need all of these different types of outfits? I shrugged away the thought and just picked out a pair of shorts and a t-shirt.

I lotioned my arms and legs and just decided to play on the computer until the day went by. Arsen mentioned my laptop in the note, but I didn't see it anywhere, which left me the only option possible. The computer in the room. Although I used this computer to play music earlier, I was still very concerned that I might stumble onto something that I should not see. That could really trigger Arsen to take my life.

I was very careful about what I clicked on. I made sure to only open the notepad application because my mind was full and I needed to write a few things down. I let some of the music play quietly while I gathered my thoughts together. I decided to start a new novel. Since my laptop was nowhere to be found and I couldn't continue working on the novel that I had already started, this could be something that I would do to pass time here. I titled it, "Locked in with Your Own Thoughts." It was going to be about a girl kept in captivity because of her bad behavior with the man she loved.

I began to type, releasing all of my thoughts.

"Forty-seven days and three hours. That's how long I've been held in captivity in the basement of my Master's house. I never knew that I could make him this angry. I never knew he would turn on me like this. It isn't too bad down here. I have a bed, a TV, and a bathroom, and there's always someone bringing me three meals a day and a couple of new books when I've finished the old ones. The only thing that's not good is the lack of human communication. I have no friends, no family, and no master.

I know you're wondering what happened, why I'm being held captive, and why I even have a master to begin with. It all started a year ago when I signed a contract with a man by the name of Eric Pierce. He is the most gorgeous man that I have ever laid eyes on, and when I first saw him at my job, I knew I wanted to be associated with him somehow.

His skin was smooth and blemish free. He wore ripped jeans, beige boots, and a long t shirt that read 'Angels set free.' He was glowing. He had such a powerful energy that I couldn't believe it. He walked around with his hands behind his back, examining the room I was in.

There was a room in the building where I worked that I used to paint in. I thought no one would ever find it, due to its hiding place, so I hung up a few of my pieces. He smiled at a few and nodded at others. He walked up to me and eyed my outfit, raising an eyebrow at my bright yellow sweater.

"Did you do all of this?" he asked.

"Yeah ...why? You going to tell on me?" I rolled my eyes and spoke in a mocking tone.

"No, none of that. I just saw this place sitting around and wanted to check it out."

I nodded and pointed to his shirt. "I love that album."

He smiled and shoved his hands in his pockets. "Same."

"So how much of my work did you see?" I asked. "And what's your name?"

"Just about all of it," he chuckled. "I'm Eric."

We spent almost an hour getting to know each other and it was beautiful.

One day after work, he stopped me at my car and told me that he'd been checking me out since he saw me. He then proceeded to ask me if I had ever participated in a dom/sub relationship.

I'd already had experience with BDSM, so I told him yes and then let him know that if he was trying to pursue this type of relationship with me then I was very much interested. He smirked and told me that he'd have a contract typed up by the next day.

The next day came and we went over the rules during lunch. One of the main rules was that I would address him, and only him, as Master. Since that day, he's been my master and I have done everything he has asked.

Exactly forty-eight days ago, I messed up. When I say I messed up, I mean it. It was really bad. Eric has been out of town for a week, and I needed sex so badly that I felt like I couldn't wait another day for him to get home. It felt as if I was going to die without it.

He came home a day early to surprise me and walked in on the worst thing ever. He caught me in the act of being with another man, and what made it worse was that I was so caught up in the moment that I called the other man Master.

The look on his face was terrifying. I had never seen him that angry or aggressive before, not even during one of our dom/sub moments. Before I knew it, I was being thrown into this basement.

"Lola." I heard Arsen's voice and jumped. I hadn't even heard the door being unlocked and opened. I had been too caught up in writing.

"Yes?" I turned to him and spoke with a slight attitude.

"What have you got there?" he raised an eyebrow and tried to look at the computer screen behind me.

"Nothing of yours, don't worry," I scoffed and crossed my arms over my chest.

"Fix your tone of voice, Lola. You're lucky I didn't kill you ... yet" He smirked and walked towards me. He handed me two spiral notebooks and a box of pens. "One book has all of the jobs you will be doing for me while you're here, and the other you can use as a journal when you get bored."

I began to read through the book and saw that there was a list of groceries that I needed to pick up tomorrow. It also mentioned that I'd get the money tomorrow and the driver would be there at ten to pick me up. Something told me that he didn't really want to punish me. It was just something about the tasks that I had to do. I mean, was grocery shopping really a task you would give to someone you were holding hostage? I didn't know. His intentions were beyond me.

"Before I go, come here." He spoke in a very demanding voice.

I got up and walked over to him. He grabbed my waist and pulled me closer to him. Our noses were barely an inch apart and he flashed a smile that made my heart melt. It felt like everything around us stopped. One of his hands grabbed the back of my neck and he kissed me. He kissed me so hard that I stopped breathing. He pulled away and chuckled, licking his lips and walking out of the room in one swift movement. Hearing the lock on the door made me snap back into reality.

That kiss just proved that someone had put the idea to kidnap me in his mind. If he was angry enough to kidnap me all on his own, he wouldn't have come in here and kissed me like that. I brushed my fingers over my bottom lip because it had begun to tingle. I wasn't sure what it was, but that kiss had felt magical. He had kissed me with so much love and passion within that three seconds that it was scary.

I didn't even get to ask him why he kissed me. I sighed and saved the document on the computer. I let the music play while I opened the window and looked at the view. I was surprised that the window wasn't nailed shut, but after looking down at the bush of thorns, I understood why. I sat on the window seat and pulled my knees to my chest.

I was bored out of my mind and had nothing better to do but watch the clouds go by and see what types of shapes they made. Besides the song playing, silence filled the air. The house, this area, the sky—it was all completely quiet. Though I had longed for this type of silence back on campus, I was starting to miss the various sounds that had surrounded me there. Being locked up, even if it had been only a couple of hours, made me miss school and my home.

I started to think about what my parents and siblings are doing at that very moment—probably playing board games or watching movies and having lunch. That's something that I'd never missed out on and I would have given anything to be doing that with them in that moment. Actually, I would have given anything to take back my horrible actions. I wish I had never looked through Arsen' emails.

Maybe I'd have a life to live.

16

ARSEN

Seeing Lola close to tears like that made me feel horrible. I couldn't believe that I'd had the chance to actually reveal my feelings for her, and instead of telling her, I kissed her. That old trick had worked on girls in the past, but I should've realized that Lola wasn't like most girls. She wasn't like the ones before. She is the one.

I tried to think quickly about how I could make her see that she was actually important to me without physically making a move on her. I started to think about how her room was lacking and that I could actually help her enjoy herself while she was here. I noticed her room had minimal entertainment in it. Al that she could enjoy herself with was the computer.

So I called up the interior designer. I told them that I needed them to do some work for me the next morning. Lola was a novelist, so clearly, she liked to read. I decided to get her a little bookshelf with a couple of books from my library. Just in case she got hungry between meals, I told the designer that I wanted a mini fridge to be put inside of the room as well. I also thought that adding a flat-screen TV to the wall wouldn't hurt. I figured she liked watching shows and movies just as much as she likes reading books.

I was really excited about this. I hoped that this would put a smile on her face while I figured out something bigger and better to do to show her that I really cared. I didn't want her to think that she was just another girl that I was playing games with. I wanted her to see truly how important she was to me. Although I had to keep her hostage, I wanted to see her nothing but happy.

Her happiness brought me joy and her smile brought me comfort. She made me feel young again and Lord knew I'd been longing for that feeling since my divorce. That was why I scheduled us to go to dinner tomorrow. I wanted to take her to a semi-normal restaurant to eat so that we could be around people of both of our age groups.

I wanted her to feel safe and secure around me. I wanted her to feel beautiful and like she was the most important girl in the world. And I knew that money could not buy her love, so I was really putting thought into this. I wanted to live the rest of my life with her. I suspected tomorrow night would be the night that I expressed my true feelings for her. I just hoped things went as planned.

Lola reminded me of the second book I had ever written. It was similar to my book that she told me she liked during our interview, but better in my opinion, as the author. This particular story didn't have an age gap between the two lovers because it was based on my ex-wife. Although I loved that woman with all of my heart, there were a few things that she could have worked on to better herself as a person.

I made sure to put those things in the novel to make it seem as though this was just a character and that her and my wife had differences. But they were good differences. The character's name was Abigail and she was Lola in the flesh. She was described the same, she talked the same, and even felt the same. It was like I was actually reliving my own book.

I smiled to myself as I continued my plans for the day. I got another strange email from the girl who may possibly have been Lola's best friend. She claimed that she knew where I lived and that she'd be sending people over to 'end' me. I chuckled and leaned back in my chair. She was a very funny girl if she thought that she could ever kill me.

I licked over my lips and started to think of ways to lure this girl in so I could retrieve her information and track her every move. Although I looked at her as a joke, threatening my life wasn't a joke and it wasn't something that I took lightly. Now my goal was to end both her life and her mother's life. I just didn't need the stress of their complaints.

I finally sent an email in response from a fake email account to let them know that things were serious:

Subject: To the mother and daughter of the man who couldn't do his job.

Let's get a few things clear. First, your threats don't scare me. As a man of wealth and people, I have nothing to fear, and if I were afraid of anything, it'd be neither of you two. I am a very hard-working man, but your loved one couldn't deliver me what I asked for. I paid him exceptionally well for minor jobs, but he still couldn't deliver what I asked for. Why? Because he was a greedy son of a bitch.

He stole money from me! It just so happens that he was the only one to come back later than the others, and he came back with less money than I requested. I was killing random people in the market because he claimed that the amount he had given me was the amount they gave him. He played with my money, so he needed to lose his life. So I'm warning you now ...if you don't stop these childish acts of trying to scare me or trying to kill me, you'll end up six feet under just like him. You rats are a disgrace.

P.S. — If you or anyone else you are associated with even puts a hand on the girl, I'll tear you to fucking pieces.

I smirked as I hit send. I felt full of energy and on edge at the moment and it was kind of crazy. I pulled out my phone and made a call to Pete to check in on everything with the group.

"Hello?" He answered. "What's up, boss man?"

"Not much," I chuckled. "How's everything looking?"

"As far as I can tell, everything is right on track. We've located the residence of the lady and we're going to handle the situation tomorrow night. Make sure you're out of the house and busy with witnesses so nothing leads back to you."

"Perfect!" I replied.

"Also, we got back the packages that were taken and more. We now dominate their shipping and get half of all of their income and profit."

"This is great." I smiled widely. Today had been the best I'd had in a while. "Where would I be without you guys?"

"We could ask the same about you, boss." I heard him laugh. "Everything will be back to normal soon.

"All right. Talk to you soon." With that, I hung up. Seemed like my life would be going smoothly again.

I was going to spend the rest of my day putting everything together for Lola and I tomorrow.

17

LOLA

I woke up yet again, but this time to a purple and orange sunset. I didn't even know that I had fallen asleep. It was like they were waiting for me to wake up, because the moment I sat up in bed, there was a knock on the door.

"Dinner." I heard Ms. Rose speak through the door. I smiled slightly, but not for long.

When the door opened, Ms. Rose wasn't alone. She walked in with a huge tray and Arsen followed swiftly behind her. I guess I wasn't eating dinner alone. I looked down at my hands and played with my fingers while Ms. Rose sat the food in front of me. I whispered a small thank you and she whispered back for me to stay strong.

I looked up only enough to see the food and Arsen's body as he took a seat on the bed. We were having grilled chicken and broccoli for dinner. I picked up my plate, placing it on my lap, and began to eat in silence. I didn't know how to feel, but I knew I wasn't necessarily in the mood to speak with Arsen right now. Especially after that kiss.

"It's a nice night, huh?" He broke the silence. I saw him take small bites of his food while waiting for my response.

I just stayed silent, not sure of how I should reply. I took another bite of my food and sat my plate to the side. I wiped my mouth with a napkin and turned away from Arsen. I went to sit on the window seat and watched the sky turn black. I heard him muffle a stiff laugh and sit his plate down on the serving tray. Then he set the tray on the dresser.

"Lola, can you talk to me please?" he asked. The sound of his feet tapping against the hardwood floor as he got closer to me made me anxious. "Why didn't you finish your dinner?"

"Not hungry," I replied simply, watching the sun almost go into hiding.

"Why are you acting like this? Is it something that I've done?" His tone of voice was dripping with concern and confusion. He took a seat beside me and I could feel his eyes burning holes into the side of my face.

"How do you actually feel about me, Arsen? Why'd you kiss me, then leave me here locked up without an explanation? Am I part of some type of sick game you're playing?" Tears began burning my eyes, waiting to fall out, but I forced them back. "Why are you doing all of this?"

"I'm not sure why I'm doing this ... but I don't want you to ever think that I'm playing you or whatever. I actually care about you." He tried to take my hand, but I quickly pulled it away. I didn't want to touch him right now.

"How do you feel about me, Arsen?" I asked again. I finally turned to face him and looked him directly in the eyes.

"I ...I can't put it into words, but I know that I can show you"

"Great." I forced out a laugh. "And how do you plan on doing that?"

He kissed me. Just leaned in and kissed me, but this time, I didn't kiss back. I stood up and walked away from him, shaking my head.

"No, Arsen. You don't get to just kiss me and leave again."

"But Lola—" He started, but I quickly interrupted.

"If you don't mind, I would really like to be alone right now"

He sighed and left the room. I heard the lock click and for some reason, it was annoyingly loud. I just wasn't quite sure how to feel at the moment. I'd had the opportunity to express my feelings for him. Better yet, he'd had the opportunity to express his feelings to me, but I guess he just wasn't ready yet.

What was crazy about the whole thing was the fact that he was a writer. It really shouldn't be that hard for him to put his feelings into words. Me being a writer as well, it was very easy for me to explain myself. I guessed it was just different for everyone.

I really needed to separate myself from him. I couldn't pinpoint this exact feeling but it was very overwhelming. I felt like I was drowning in a sea of my own emotions and I was too far away to swim back to shore. This was what I called the visionary aspect of a writer's mind. I had these moments where I actually envisioned my thoughts and my imagination became so vivid that it felt real.

The color blue surrounded me, but it surrounded me in various shades. Both warm and cool tones captured my soul in a way they hadn't before. Blue sky, blue clouds, and blue waves. There was fog everywhere and the air was clammy. My hair stuck to my arms like feeding leeches.

It was not salty ocean water that I was floating in. I was washing away in my own tears. I took a look up and the clouds looked like question marks. They had this gold glow that rested around the edges of their shape like they were hiding the answer to all this confusion from me.

The sky turned a peachy orange color as my body washed up onto a black sand beach. After seconds of coughing up water, I started to catch my breath. The sun peeked through the clouds letting me know that even though things may have seemed solely negative at the moment, things were going to be okay. Left in the sand were the footprints of another human being who was now vacant. I wondered if they were on the same trail of vivid emotions.

I was just trying to find my way through this warped reality but I knew that it would take a while. It was already taking me a while to process the thought of Arsen not feeling the same as I did, but what if he didn't feel anything for me at all? What if this was just a simple scam for him to have his way with me and still end up killing me in the end. I didn't know. I didn't think he wanted to kill me, but with him, I never knew his true intentions until he acted upon them.

Why did I feel like the only one who didn't have the answers? Why must I be the one lost at sea?

My questions almost never had answers to them and I wished I knew why. It had almost always seemed like the answers to my questions would only come in the form of a conclusion to my overall problem, which was very annoying because the situation could last for years and I would be confused all the way up until the very end, when things were solved. I threw myself onto the bed and pulled the blanket over me. It felt like I was a child again.

When I was younger, I would always crawl into bed and lay under my blankets as a way to solve my problems. It was the place that made me feel safe and that was why, for the longest period of time, my room was my sacred place. Being alone in there made it so easy to be one with my thoughts.

It had been only a few seconds, but within that short amount of time, I felt like I was in my sacred place again. But this wasn't my home and I didn't think it ever would be. I knew that my feelings for Arsen were very strong, but I just didn't know if he felt the same. I didn't even know if his kisses were genuine. I needed him to show me that he actually cared for me in more ways than just physical.

There were a million and one ways that he could express his love for me, if he had any, but he'd just have to find out how to show me on his own. If he felt the same way, this wouldn't be a problem. Although I had just taken a nap, I decided to just go back to sleep and get ready for whatever Arsen had planned for me to do tomorrow.

I woke up to the loud ringing of the alarm clock, which was crazy, because I didn't even set it. I pushed myself out of bed and into the bathroom to take care of my hygiene. My schedule said that this morning I would be grocery shopping and that I should be ready to leave by 9:45 so that I could make it to the store by opening time.

It was just grocery shopping, so I decided to wear a t-shirt, a pair of yoga pants, and a pair of running shoes. At 9:45 sharp, the door unlocked and opened. In front of me stood Ms. Rose and Arsen's driver.

"Are you ready, Lola?" Ms. Rose asked.

"Yes," I said with a smile, then she handed me the grocery list and the credit card.

"You can follow me to the car, Ms. Lola," the driver spoke. His smile never left his face the entire time.

I followed him out to the car, got inside, and he opened the door for me. I was happy to be out in the fresh air after being locked up in the house for a day and a half. I rolled down my window and let the wind blow through my hair as we drove off. I tucked the grocery list and card into my back pocket, trying to clear my mind off the task that needed to be done until it was actually time to do it.

We drove through part of town that I had never seen before. This must have been where the wealthy people shopped because the buildings around the other parts of the city were nowhere near as nice as these. The driver found a perfect parking space right in front of the grocery store and told me that he would be waiting for me right in this spot when I was finished. I thanked him and got out.

The store was named Organic Everything. It was set up really nicely and organized throughout the entire store. I grabbed a cart and pulled out the list of items that I needed to pick up. Finding things in the store was very easy, due to how they labeled everything from the aisles to the prices. Strangely, this brought me peace.

The soft music playing from the ceiling speakers and the subtle chill that surrounded me put me at ease. I wouldn't mind doing this all of the time. This felt like meditation.

I had gotten all of the items that were on the list within fifteen minutes. Just when I was about to close the note and put it away, I saw something written at the bottom. It told me to also pick up a few of my favorite snacks, because by the time I got back I would have a mini fridge and a small cabinet for my items.

I smiled at the list and put it away before quickly doing another run of the store and picking up a few things that I wouldn't mind snacking on from time to time. I went to the cashier and paid for all of the items. Maybe this day would be better than yesterday.

The driver helped me pack the groceries into the trunk and we both got back inside of the car. I kept my snacks in the back-seat with me. The music on the radio was playing little louder than it had been earlier, and it was on another station too. It was on the alternative station, and I knew every song that came on back-to-back. This was just another good thing to add on to this good day.

When we got back to the house, the driver told me to just take my personal bags up to my room and that he would take care of the rest. I thanked him and went inside of the house. There was a guard waiting for me at the bottom of the stairs, and as much as I should be upset that I was going to be locked inside of his room for the rest of the day, I wasn't. I was happy and I didn't think anything could ruin my happiness right then.

The guard let me into the room and locked the door behind me. Just like the note said, there were a mini cabinet and a mini fridge. There was also a slender bookshelf full of books in the corner. The smile on my face got bigger and I felt the happiest I'd been in a few weeks. Who would have thought pure happiness could come from being locked in captivity?

I thought it was really nice that Arsen took the time out of his day to do those things for me. I guessed this was him showing that he appreciated me. That gave me a little reassurance. I smiled to myself and put the snacks away. When I turned around, I jumped a little at what randomly appeared. There was a TV mounted on the wall and I'm not sure how I missed it upon entering. There was a sticky note attached to it.

I walked closer to the TV, and the note read:

"I'm sorry about last night. I hope you can forgive me"

I shook my head and took the note off of the TV screen. I tossed it into the small trash bin and walked back over to the bed to sit down. He didn't have to buy me gifts to apologize, but I did appreciate the things he gave me. They could entertain me while I was locked up in here, however long that would be.

Luckily for me, I saw a couple of books that I'd been meaning to read on the bookshelf. So that was another great thing to look forward to. I got up and sat in front of the computer. I was going to write a little more of my story.

I know you're wondering what my name is, and I'll tell you. My name is Hazel and I fell in love with my dominant. He fell in love with me too, but his feelings aren't there anymore. Not since I hurt his feelings. I used to make him so happy. I love his smile. It's the most beau-

tiful thing in the world. I can't believe that I even brought myself to hurt such a beautiful soul like that.

I remember waking up every day to make him breakfast and to make sure his clothes were ironed for work. I just miss making him happy. Being trapped down here in the basement gives me enough time to think and, man, have I learned my lesson. Never take the one you love for granted.

18

ARSEN

It was finally time for us to go out and I was nothing but happy. I pulled out one of my best suits and put extra effort into doing my hair. I knocked on her door and waited for her response. After a few moments, I didn't hear anything, so I just unlocked the door and let myself in. Her music was playing faintly in the corner of the room and I heard things moving around in the bathroom.

"Lola?" I called, tapping my knuckles against the bathroom door slightly.

"Almost ready!" she called out.

"All right. Meet me downstairs when you're done, love."

"Okay." I heard her giggle and it touched my heart. I smiled and let out a small chuckle.

I left her door unlocked and went downstairs at the end of the stairs to wait for her. I knew she was just going to be beautiful beyond words. My heart raced as I waited for her to be in my presence. She headed downstairs and I was taken aback by her breathtaking beauty.

I smiled and took her hand, helping her down the last few stairs. My eyes traced her body as I admired her outfit. She had on an all-white, long-sleeved dress with rose gold jewelry and matching rose gold heels. Her makeup looked amazing and her hair was pulled up into a bun.

"You look absolutely stunning, Lola." I smiled and pulled her closer to me.

She draped her arms around my neck and pulled me into a hug. I smelled her natural scent, but it'd been enhanced. Her aura opened my senses a little more. She pulled away slowly and smiled at me.

"Ready to go?" I asked and she nodded, sliding her hand back into mine.

I led her out to the car and opened the door for her. We both got in and I closed the door behind us. The driver pulled off, and he began taking the long way. I wanted Lola to see the entire city in one night. Instead of cutting through town, we took the highway, which surrounds the city. You could see all of the buildings and bright lights in action, and it was up closer than the view from my place.

Her face lit up when she saw everything, especially the harbor. I saw the twinkle in her eye when she saw the tall Ferris wheel. Little did she know I already had that planned for after we had our dinner.

I felt like a teenager again, out late at night with the girl of my dreams. For that moment in time, it felt as if we were the only two people on earth. I looked over at her, just taking in the beauty of her surroundings, and felt my feelings becoming even stronger.

We made it to the restaurant and it wasn't crowded. This made me ten times happier than before. We were escorted to a table that was in the middle of everyone. The people surrounding us looked like everyday people, which is exactly what I wanted. I wanted Lola to know that there would be times when we could hang out and still be around normal citizens.

"How are you feeling tonight, beautiful?" I asked Lola. "You look absolutely stunning."

"Why, thank you, Arsen." She blushed. Her cheeks became a rosy pink color and she flashed a childish grin. "I'm feeling amazing tonight. Thank you for bringing me out."

I nodded. "I just want the night to be special for you. For us."

I wanted tonight to be memorable for the both of us. I wanted us to express our love for each other and hopefully take a big step forward with what we have between us.

"I'm really honored to be here right now. It's really comforting seeing average people here tonight, and the fact that you are here with just me and no guards is amazing. You're a billionaire with a crazy woman after you. You're so brave and I admire that." Lola spoke, pulling her chair closer to the table.

"If anyone should be honored, it should be me. I'm sitting face-to-face with an angel right now and I couldn't be any more grateful." I smiled and grabbed her hand, placing a kiss on it.

I felt like I was on top of the world. It was like time slowed down, but we were still in the present. The only thing I cared about in that moment was me and her. I would love for her to really give me a chance. I'd been sitting there the entire time, thinking about the right thing to say to her. Maybe something along the lines of:

"Lola, I know we've only known each other for a short while now, but I'm falling fast and I'm falling hard. My feelings for you are starting to become so unbearable that, if I don't tell you, I'll lose my mind. You may not feel the same and that's okay, because we are still in the process of getting to know each other, but if you could just give me a chance, I won't disappoint you. I can promise you that I can make you happy and I can provide you with the things that you want and need. I don't want you to look at this as me trying to bribe you with money or materialistic things, because giving you everything that you want and need doesn't just apply to luxurious items. I can satisfy you mentally, physically, and emotionally. If you could just let me show you how much you mean to me, this could be the start of something new and amazing."

"Hi, my name's—" the waitress began, but was quickly cut off by Lola.

"Anabella?!" Lola shouted.

"Lola?" the waitress questioned as she raised an eyebrow. She turned to me and her face turned into a look of disgust and hate. Bingo. This had to be the daughter of that awful man who had worked for me, who also happened to be Lola's best friend.

"Anabella," I smirked.

"You," she spat, and before I could blink she lunged towards me.

A BILLIONAIRE'S STRENGTH

An Alpha Billionaire Romance

By Michelle Love

19

LOLA

"Anabella," Arsen smirked. He looked as if he was reaching him out to introduce himself. I kind of smiled at how nice he was being.

"You," Anabella spat. She began to lunge towards Arsen, and thankfully, there a worker nearby watching the entire situation. Before she touched Arsen, the other waiter hooked an arm around her body and snatched her back.

"I'm so sorry about that, Mr. Lockhart!" The waiter apologized to Arsen and pulled Anabella away, leaving me shocked and Arsen very confused.

"What was that all about?" My eyes widened in disbelief. "W-why would she even do a thing like that?"

"I have no idea." Arsen sat up straight in his seat and shrugged his shoulders. "Did I do something?"

. . .

"No." I shook my head. "She's just been acting really strangely since I met you. I think the fact that I may be paying more attention to you than her may have gotten into her head a little too much."

"That's unfortunate." Arsen spoke with a saddened tone. He sounded really genuine and I couldn't believe Anabella would even be that upset about what was going on between us.

"Yeah ..." I sighed and looked down at the menu. "You probably want to leave, don't you? I can't believe she just ruined everything!"

"No, no, no. Not at all"

My head shot up and I saw a smile on his face. I felt my heart melt. "Really?"

"Yeah. I'm not going to let a little incident like that ruin our night. I planned this night specifically for us and no one's going to come between that." His smile got bigger.

"Well, then." I smiled back at him, picking up my menu and nodding. "What do you plan on eating?"

. . .

"Let's find out" He let out a small chuckle and picked up his menu, scanning over it with his eyes.

I couldn't do much but blush. I couldn't believe that something extreme had just happened, but we were still here enjoying ourselves.

The waiter came back to our tables and introduced himself, apologizing once more for what had happened with Anabella. I nodded along with Arsen, and we proceeded to order our meals.

"So, I have an interview with this magazine for novelists and they want me to bring someone along with me who's a great writer." He smiled.
"That's so cool!" I exclaimed. "Who are you going to take?"

"You."

My mouth dropped. M-me? Out of all writers, why me? I mean, I completely agreed that I deserved the opportunity, but how did he even know if I were a good writer or not?

"Why me?" I raised an eyebrow. The waiter came back with two waters and a plate of lemons. I dropped two slices of lemon into my water and swirled them around with my straw.

. . .

"I forgot to mention that whatever is saved on the computer in your room automatically syncs to every other computer in the house." He chuckled.

My mouth dropped again, opening wider than before. That meant he had read the story that I had begun to write about the girl betraying her 'master' and being thrown into a basement under lock and key. I wondered if he noticed that the story slightly related to the situation between us.

"Don't worry," he laughed. "I loved your story, and honestly, I think you're an amazing writer. The way you write is similar to the way I write and I think you'd be perfect for the interview."

"Wow. Thank you so much, Arsen!" I smiled and took a sip from my water. Could this night get any better? This could be my big break for my career. What better way to celebrate than with the man who made it all happen?

I wondered what the rest of the night had in store for us. I would have never seen all of this coming a couple of weeks ago, but I'm glad it came as a surprise. It was crazy how the one time I decided to do something that I shouldn't, I was introduced to a man who could change my life forever. God, what did I do to be this lucky?

We began to eat soon as the food got to the table. We must have both been starving. Arsen ordered the steak with rice and asparagus, and I ordered a hearty salad with a side of mixed veggies. I wanted to stay light on the stomach. He began to talk, going on about something, but I wasn't paying attention because I got lost in his eyes.

They glistened in the restaurant's light as he continued to speak.

"Are you okay with that?" he asked.

"Um ...yeah," I said, not really knowing what he was asking me. I didn't want him to know that I hadn't been paying attention. Whatever I had agreed to couldn't have been that bad.

"Great!" He smiled and finished up his meal. I did the same.

Arsen paid for the meal and we left. When we got back inside of the car, the driver pulled off in the direction of Arsen's home. I frowned a bit, not really wanting the night to be over with.

I looked out of the window and watched as others walked hand and hand through the city streets. It made me happy. I hoped that Arsen and I could be like that someday soon. I looked over at him and he was staring directly at me.

"What?" I laughed. "Is there something on my face?"

"No." He stated bluntly, with a mild expression. "You're just really beautiful, Lola."

"Thanks." I blushed, brushing a piece of flyaway hair behind my ear. "You're beautiful too, Arsen."

"I know."

We both looked at each other and laughed. He was doing a good job of keeping me amused tonight. Other times he had been very pushy, but tonight he'd been really laid back and I appreciated that.

We took the highway back toward Arsen's house, but I noticed the driver took an unexpected turned. I turned to Arsen to see if he had noticed, but he didn't seem to care.

We soon pulled up to the harbor and my eyes lit up. I'd always wanted to go, but never did. I felt myself become very excited, like a child in a toy store. The lights were bright and lit up everything around us. What made everything better was that it was right on the beach. The waves were crashing and couples were making their way toward the water as the sun began to go down.

When the driver came to a stop, Arsen got out and jogged around the car to open the door for me. I stepped out and grabbed Arsen's hand, pulling myself closer to him. I looked over the harbor in amazement.

He led me down a path over to a stand. We walked hand in hand under the trees. He bought me two roses from the florist at the stand, one red and one white.

"Thank you for all of this, Arsen." I smiled.

"Anything for you, princess," he mumbled in a low but audible tone.

I felt my cheeks burn red. I didn't know why I got so shy and child-like around him. We walked down to another stand where he bought me cotton candy. I didn't know exactly where we were heading, but I hoped it was somewhere great. He led me to yet another stand, but that time bought me a teddy bear. It was red and white, just like the roses.

We continued walking down the same path and Arsen told me to close my eyes. I closed my eyes and walked with him slowly to our destination. I felt a gush of wind blow across my face as I felt him guide me on to some type of seat. I sat there with my eyes closed and I felt him sit beside me. He was rather close, too. I heard what sounded like metal clamping together and that completely erased my thoughts of us being inside of the building.

"You can open your eyes now, Lola," Arsen said softly, and I felt us begin to move.

. . .

I opened my eyes and saw that I was on a Ferris wheel. I clapped my hands together in excitement and flashed a big smile at Arsen.

"I saw the way you looked at it on the way to the restaurant and figured that I couldn't miss out on the opportunity to see that smile on your face. The exact smile that you have on your face right now. I know this will be a great decision." He smiled at me and took my hand into his.

"You've made me so happy tonight. I don't know how I could repay you." I stared him directly in the eyes.

"You don't have to pay me back. This night is about you." He said, while taking a piece of my cotton candy.

I laughed and looked out at the sunset. The sky was various shades of pink, orange, and purple. As the sky was going dark slowly and the Ferris wheel was heading up toward the sky, I started to drift off into a deep thought.

Was I getting in way over my head or was I actually falling for this guy? It was just a simple date, but it was just the way that he went about things that made this more than ordinary. Everything about him, besides him being a murderer, was perfect. It was sort of scary. He could kill me at any time and get away with it, but for some reason that was completely okay with me.

. . .

I felt wild, carefree, and reckless when I was with Arsen. I wanted this feeling to last forever, but I'd have to wait a little to see if the feelings are real or if it was just lust.

"Lola."

"Huh?" I came back to reality and looked over at him.

"We're back on the ground." He chuckled and opened the metal door for us to get out. We got out and started to walk toward the beach. The walk gave me just enough time to eat my cotton candy. I shared most of it with Arsen because I wasn't that big into sweets. I held the stuffed bear and roses close to my body as we neared the water.

"Beautiful, isn't it?" Arsen asked, referring to the now-dark sky and sparkling stars.

I nodded in agreement and took off my heels. I sat the bear and roses next to them and walked toward the ocean, letting the water come up to my calves. I pulled my bun down and loosened my hair, letting the soft wind blow through it.

Serenity. I felt pure serenity.

"You are absolutely stunning." Arsen took me by the hand and spun me around. Was this a fairytale? It felt like it.

. . .

I FELT Arsen's hands slide around my waist and pull me close. He rested his chin on my shoulder and took a deep breath. All I could do was smile. I couldn't find the words to say. I didn't have any words to say. I just wanted to take in everything at the moment.

WHO KNEW the next time this would happen again? I laid my hands on top of his and looked out at the stars once more. I felt him place small kisses on my neck and I tensed up.

"LET'S GO, BEAUTIFUL." He spoke under his breath, but clear enough for me to hear. He walked away to get my things. I slid on my heels and followed behind Arsen like a lost child. Funny how he made me feel like a child and a grown woman at the same time.

When we made it back to entrance, the driver was waiting for us. It was odd. I never knew if he waited outside of places for us the entire time or if Arsen texted or called him. I laughed a little and got inside of the car.

THE DRIVER HAS classical music playing softly and it actually put me at ease. I laid my back against the seat and felt myself begin to doze off.

20

ARSEN

We made it back to the house and Lola was fast asleep. She looked so beautiful, but she was so unaware of it. She looked like a fallen angel. I smiled slightly and rested her roses and teddy bear in her lap. I scooped her up in my arms and went inside. I took the elevator up to her room and took her inside, laying her in her bed. The room was loaded with flowers that I had delivered while we were out.

I WANTED TO UNDRESS HER, but the moment between us was just so ...innocent. Though I wasn't planning on doing anything sexual to her, I still wanted my first time seeing her fully naked to be with her consent.

I JOGGED to the bathroom and got a washcloth. I brought it back and gently wiped off her makeup. I smiled at the view of her bare face and threw the now-dirty cloth in the hamper. I called

Ms. Rose upstairs to change her out of her clothes and into a gown so that she could sleep comfortably.

When she made it to the room, I left and went to my room. I sat on the bed and sighed, rubbing my hands over my face. What was I feeling? I asked myself that every day, but I really needed answers. Even with women I found myself really liking, I had sex with them the first night and maybe even before we got the chance to go on a date.

But with Lola, everything was different. Of course, I lusted after her, but I just wanted to wait until she was ready. I wanted to wait for the right time for the both of us in general. She was special and I didn't want to lose her.

I took a quick shower and slid on a fresh pair of sweats. With only the light of the moon and stars shining in my room, I went to sleep.

I woke up the next day without a care in the world. It was my day off from everything—the cartel, the office, etc. I didn't really know what to do, so I just sat in the bed thinking about the night before.

Her skin was flawless and so was her smile. I didn't think she had any imperfections other than being nosey and looking through my emails. I shook my head, thinking back to why I'd had to lock her back in her room. I didn't quite know if I was ready to let her free just yet. When I had told her at dinner, she seemed completely okay with it.

. . .

I grabbed my phone and texted David, giving him all of the details about what happened with Anabella. I told him that we now knew that worker's daughter's name and that we could use his last name to track her and her mother down. Just thinking about how she had lunged at me like that pissed me off. Who did she think she was? What did she think she was going to do to me? Choke me to death? Ha!

Did she know who she was fucking with?! I got angry just thinking about it. I decided to go to the gym I had built in my basement to blow off some steam.

21

LOLA

I woke up in bed, dressed in night clothing again. I must be a really hard sleeper, because I never felt it when I was changed or carried to bed. I looked at the clock and it was 8:13 on the dot. I finally looked around the room and there were multiple bouquets of roses around the room, some white and some red. I blushed and pushed myself out of bed.

I walked over to roses and smelled them. They smelled absolutely beautiful and they put me in an even better mood than before. I looked over at the window seat and there was a huge box of black roses with a note attached. It read:

Dear Lola,

Last night was beautiful and I hope we can share more experiences like that. You bring out a side of me that hasn't been out in a while. Thank you so much for that. I hope these flowers can show you a little of how I feel.

Enjoy, princess.

Arsen

I felt on top of the world in that moment. I just wanted to hug and kiss him! I skipped over to the door and turned the knob, but it barely moved because it was locked. My eyebrows knitted together in confusion.

We'd had such a good night together. I didn't see why he would still keep me locked in the room. I rolled my eyes and went into the bathroom to take a shower.

I let the warm water run through my hair and down my body. It relaxed me instantly and let me think clearly. I began thinking back to dinner, when I absentmindedly agreed to something that I hadn't heard Arsen say.

Maybe I had agreed to continue being locked away in this room. I sighed and got out of the shower, drying myself. I went to the closet and threw on some sweats and a sports bra.

I opened the journal I was given, with all my tasks inside, and saw that I had nothing to do that day. I shrugged and decided to work on more of my story since I had that interview with Arsen soon.

He has the most beautiful mind I have ever come across. I know that after just a couple of months he is becoming much more than just a dominant to me. I am falling for him. And he is falling for me too. It was kind of cool, because it was just strictly BDSM and a contract at first, then it stemmed into a strong relationship because of the bond we have.

I remember when it happened. We had just finished up a session, and while we were getting dressed, he offered to take me out to dinner the next night. Of course, I agreed. With a gorgeous man like that I couldn't pass up the offer.

His personality was amazing and so charming that I developed a huge crush on him. Before that night it was just lust, but after I got to know him a little better, we really connected and it turned into the best relationship I've ever been in.

I had basically just described my feelings for Arsen. I wondered if we would read it later on. I hoped that he would read through the lines and see what I was saying about him. I shut off the computer and went over to my bed to watch some TV.

I appreciated what I had done the previous night with Arsen, and I definitely loved the roses. It was a brand-new day and I wished that there was something for me to do other than lying around. If this had been the weekend, back when I was in school, then I would have totally been okay with watching movies, reading a book, or writing. But it was the summer and I wanted to have fun.

I needed to find a way to be closer to him, but also to have a life of my own. After a few minutes of thinking, I knew exactly what I was going to do.

22

ARSEN

About three days had gone by and I hadn't spoken to Lola. I knew that her schedule had been rather empty, but I was going to change that. I was going to do a little shopping and I wanted to take her along with me. I went to her bedroom and I knocked on the door.

"Yes? I'm not exactly able to open the door, but who is it?" I heard her voice through the door.

"It's Arsen. I'm coming in." I unlocked her door and went in. She was tucked under the blanket, reading a book. She looked so adorable. "I'm going to the mall and I want you to come with me"

"Okay. Um, how should I dress?" she asked, lifting her head from the book and turning to look at me.

"Just something simple and comfortable." I replied. "I'm leaving your door unlocked. Come get me from my room when you're ready"

She nodded and got out of bed, walking into the closet. I quickly left, making sure to leave her door unlocked, and went back to my bedroom to change out of my sweats. I took a quick shower and threw on a t-shirt and jeans. I also decided to wear a pair of shades and a hat. Believe it or not, but people failed to realize who I was in that simple disguise.

As I sprayed on cologne, I heard a knock on the bedroom door. When I answered it, it was Lola. She was wearing a nice flowy blouse with jeans and flats. I already knew that people were going to view me as some type of sugar daddy, although I look really great for my age. It was something about the ponytail and soft makeup that made Lola look younger than she actually was. Maybe it was because she wasn't wearing her signature bold red lipstick.

But at that moment, I couldn't care less what anyone had to say about us. All I knew was that I was having fun and spending time with a girl—no, woman—that I really liked. I knew we were going to get stares from various people, and I didn't have a problem with that, but I did take those feelings into consideration. She was tough enough to handle it, but that didn't mean that she was comfortable with it. This was going to be in the back of my mind the entire time we were out.

"You ready to go?" I asked.

"Born ready," she replied with a smile on her face and turned to walk down the hall. She could make the simplest things so cute and attractive. It was amazing.

I decided to drive us to the mall myself, instead of getting a new driver, because I wanted this to feel more personal. I wanted to show her that I was putting thought into our outings and also show her that not everything was fancy and professional when it came to me. I opened the door for her and closed it after she got in. I smiled to myself and spun the keys around my finger while walking around to the driver's seat. Today was going to be a great day.

While driving to the mall, we both sang along to the classical rock songs that played on the radio. It was cool to know that she was into the same music that I was, and that she actually knew about these older songs in the first place.

We finally made it to the mall and I parked in a specific spot that was usually more convenient for me. It was a place off in the corner of the parking garage, which is right next to the elevator that led to the store that I liked the most. We both got out and got on the elevator going up to the second floor. As soon as the door opened, I led her straight across the mall to the store that I needed to go into. It was a menswear store.

I needed something new to wear for the interview and I was sure that Lola could help me find something. My mother always told me that a woman's opinion could go a long way and I believed that since I was a child. And while all women may not be the best, the nicest, or the most intelligent, their opinions on different things can give you the answers that you need. That was why I went to Ms. Rose with a lot of the problems that I had. Not only was she trustworthy, but she'd been with me for so long and her knowledge and wisdom had gotten me through some of my toughest times.

"Can you help me pick out a suit to wear to the interview?" I asked, looking over at Lola.

"Sure." She smiled and walked further into the store. I walked behind her until she made a sudden stop. "Is there anything specific you're looking for?"

"No, not at all."

"Hmm." Index finger against her chin, she walked over toward a dark grey suit. "This would look amazing with a red tie."

"You think so?" I asked, smirking and holding the suit up to my body.

"I do," she stated bluntly. "It's a bit slenderer than what you usually wear and it will definitely make you stand out. You have the perfect body for it."

"Well then I'm buying it." I smiled and took it to the cash register. Lola followed behind me with a silk red tie in hand.

After paying for my things and leaving, I wanted to take Lola to get something that she wanted.

"Do you see anything that you like around here? Better yet, what were you planning on wearing to the interview?" I asked.

"I was thinking about wearing a nice dress with a blazer, a pair of heels, and a nice necklace and watch combination. Maybe even some rings." She looked really passionate about what she was planning to wear and I loved it.

Any other time I'd taken someone out shopping, they had acted shy and claimed that they didn't know what they wanted, that they didn't know the type of clothing they were into, or that I should choose for them. It was kind of weird that girls would even act that way around me. I knew that I had a lot of money, but I'd always made women feel comfortable enough to be bold and straight up with me. Or at least I thought I had.

"I think I might know the perfect store. My treat. Get whatever you want," I said, and she followed me around the mall. We finally made it to a women's wear store which was more modern, so I thought that would be perfect for her. I knew she wouldn't like to go shopping in a store for women much older than her.

We walked inside and she didn't hesitate to go directly to whatever she wanted or whatever caught her eye. I liked that. I loved a woman who knew what she wanted. She picked up a few things and two blazers.

"Follow me," she said as she walked to the dressing room. I followed her to the main area of the fitting rooms, where there were seats. I sat down and waited for her to come out and show me whatever she chose to try on first.

She came out in a lilac-colored dress that was fitted at the top but flared out at the bottom. She had decided to put the white blazer over top of that.

"What do you think about this?" she asked, spinning around the circle.

"Personally, I think you look super adorable in it. That's not what we want. You're a grown woman and that needs to be shown in this interview." I spoke in complete honesty and she nodded in agreement.

"I'm glad you said that because the next two options are just that." She went back inside of the dressing room to try on the second option.

The next time she came out wearing a long-sleeved, knee-length, fitted dress that was black. She covered that with the same white blazer that she had tried on before. She lifted an eyebrow and waited for my response.

"Now this ..." I paused. "This is beautiful, Lola. The only thing that I don't like about it is that it's a little bland. We need something that will really catch the interviewer's eye. It's going to be recorded and broadcasted on their website."

She nodded again, but this time she didn't say anything in return. I waited a little longer this time. I scrolled through my phone, sending a few short texts, until I saw a pair of legs stand in front of me. I looked up at Lola in complete awe. She was wearing a red jumpsuit with a dark grey blazer. It was perfect, and I didn't know if she did it on purpose, but it matched the outfit that she had picked out for me to wear.

"This is the one." I nodded. "We're getting it."

"I knew you'd like it. That's why I saved it for last." She giggled and left to go put her clothes back on.

When she came back out, I helped her pick out the jewelry she said she was going to wear, and she picked out a nice pair of heels. I paid for everything and we were on our way. I started going downstairs where there were more stores and the food court.

"Where are we going next?" Lola trailed behind me like a lost puppy.

"Well, you can't go to the interview without a new bag, can you?" Her eyes lit up and she smiled from ear to ear.

"You really are the best, Arsen. Thank you so much." I felt her fingers slide between mine as we were walking side by side.

The thing I mentioned earlier, about people staring at us, neither of us bothered to look, nor did we care to. We were both having a great time and we were cherishing that moment between us. I never knew if I would feel like this again. I never thought the pain of heartbreak that I had felt for the last seven or eight years would subside all in the name of a twenty-one-year-old. Quite the gap, but age shouldn't matter as long as it's legal.

I swear, every time I was with the woman I fell harder for her. Her personality, her confidence, and her elegance inside and out. She was a woman of pure beauty, and I knew I had to have her. She was like a book that I couldn't put down.

We made it into the store to get her a new bag and her eyes opened wide. I knew that there are a lot to choose from, so I whispered in her ear to get three different types of bags.

"Thank you so much!" She stood on her toes to give me a kiss on the cheek. She wandered off around the store, looking at different bags that caught her eye, and I walked behind her slowly, just admiring her beauty and her excitement. I knew a lot of men had a problem shopping with a woman because they found it boring, but honestly, I found it relaxing.

How could you not love watching your woman do something that made her happy? Even if it was not your thing or your hobbies, why be negative about it? A woman that you like or love is genuinely happy and you complain because it's not what you want to do? I couldn't relate.

I paid for the three bags she chose and we started to walk toward the food court.

"Do you know what you want to eat?"

"Chinese," she answered. "It's my favorite thing to get while I'm out shopping. What are you having?"

"Chinese. It's your favorite, so I'll have what you have" I smiled and held my hand out for her to lead the way.

She blushed and made her way over to the Chinese restaurant. It was one of those all-you-can-eat places, but cleaner and with better food because of the area of the city we were shopping in. I paid for our entry and got both our plates, looking around for what we were going to eat. I stuck with vegetable lo mein and spring rolls, while Lola got orange chicken and steamed rice with vegetables on the side.

I didn't eat Chinese food that often, but I had a craving for it that day because it looked so good. We went back to our seats and began eating. It was silent for a few minutes, just the sound of chewing between us, until Lola spoke up.

"I have something to tell you," she said as she looked down at her plate, pushing a piece of chicken around with her fork.

"What is it, love?" I put a forkful of lo mein into my mouth and began to chew it up.

"I want to help you with the drug cartel." She dropped her fork onto the plate and looked up at me.

"What?" I nearly choked on my food and hurried to swallow it. "What do you mean you want to help?"

"I want to be a part of it. I want to help you. I know that this means a lot to you and that you're still working on trying to trust me again, but this could really help. If I'm a part of the cartel, telling someone could get me in trouble too." She smiled sneakily.

"Uh, I don't know about that. This is a very dangerous business and I wouldn't want you getting hurt." I took a sip of my drink and sat up in my seat, looking at her. She had a point about her taking the fall as well if this secret were to ever get out.

"I don't care, Arsen. I want to be a part of this and I want to help you. Even if I'm doing work behind the scenes and no one knows who I am. It'll be like anonymous work ...you know?" She took a few more bites of her food and waited for my response.

"Are you sure about this, Lola?" I raised an eyebrow.

"Yes! Now tell me what I have to do." She smirked and finished her plate of food.

23

LOLA

I was glad to have finally been able to leave the house, to be able to get new things, to be treated like a princess, and to top it all off ...for my plan to work. Yes, my plan to be closer to Arsen and to not always be trapped inside of that room had begun. Working with a cartel had its pro's and con's, but the way my life was looking, I didn't seem to have that much of an option.

"Yes! Now tell me what I have to do." I smirked and finished my plate of food. Maybe my tasks within this cartel wouldn't be that big of a deal.

"We should go home first before we discuss this topic any further." Arsen spoke under his breath. He finished his meal and took a sip of his drink.

I flashed a small smile to let him know that I understood. We grabbed our bags and left, getting on the same elevator that let us off right in front of Arsen's car. I didn't notice until we pulled out that the parking spot actually had the name "Lockhart" painted on it in big, yellow letters.

I CHUCKLED and rolled my window down. I felt the breeze push my ponytail toward the left, to where it hit Arsen's arm. I laughed at the overly-dramatic look of annoyance on his face and pulled my ponytail into a low bun. I tied an extra hair tie around it to keep it secure.

THERE WAS SILENCE BETWEEN US, but it was a comfortable silence. The radio still played those classic rock songs and we were just cruising. I liked the fact that he wasn't in a rush to get home. It made me feel like he did in fact feel the same way I did, somewhat.

THIS MARKED the start of some crazy adventure that I was about to get myself into. But who cared? I was young and I felt even younger. This was the excitement that I had been craving since I turned twenty years old. I never expected for an older man to bring out the youth within me, but that was exactly what happened. He brought out a side of me that had become very foreign. My wild side was starting to show.

When we made it onto the highway, Arsen pulled the roof of his car back and turned the music up louder. He began picking up speed and swerving past other cars.

"DID YOU ENJOY YOURSELF, TODAY?" Arsen asked.

. . .

"I DID!" I giggled. "Thank you so much for taking me out, and also, thanks for the new things!"

HE SMILED AND NODDED.

SUDDENLY, I had a flashback to when we first went out.

I' was twenty-one years old and I had butterflies before going on a date. Nothing wrong with that. I just always thought life would turn out differently for me. Maybe that was why I' was so open with Arsen. It might not seem like it on his end, but I didn't even give guys the time of day, so he was lucky. I felt like he could be that missing excitement that I needed in my life. I was just so used to being by myself without any distractions. I wasn't sure if a relationship was what I needed right now, but I was willing to try it out.

MY PHONE LIT UP, *showing a text from Arsen. It said that he was outside and that his driver was waiting for me. I laughed a little and slid on my shoes. I didn't even know why I would have expected a billionaire to drive himself to a restaurant. I made it outside and saw the driver open the back door. I kindly thanked him and got inside. Arsen sat, watching me get in the car with a smile on his face. His teeth were the whitest I'd ever seen. All of his teeth were perfectly straight. It was mesmerizing.*

"YOU LOOK ABSOLUTELY STUNNING, LO," *he spoke.*

"Thank you. You look good as well, Arsen." I blushed slightly at the nickname he had given me.

The ride there was lovely. I got to see the view of downtown at night while music played softly in the background. The air was fresh while blowing through my hair. I felt like my nineteen-year-old self again. I heard a chuckle and turned to see Arsen watching me.

This adrenaline rush within me caused various flashbacks.

Before I could even make it to the door, Arsen stepped in and closed it behind him. "Did you ...find all that you were looking for on the computer?"

I gulped and nodded. "I'll just be leaving now."

When I tried to walk past him, he grabbed my wrist, and I felt myself being pushed against the wall. I gasped and looked up at Arsen, who was now hovering over me. I could tell by the look on his face that I was caught and this wasn't going to be easy.

"You know, it's really not polite to go through people's emails. You don't have the right," he spat.

"I don't know what you're talking about—" I mumbled and was quickly cut off.

"Don't play stupid with me, Lola. I was standing in the doorway the entire time," he scoffed.

"Arsen, I swear—" I was cut off again.

"I know what you saw on that computer and you don't know how much trouble you're in now, Lola. But you don't seem like the type to be a loud mouth about these type of things, so I'm considering letting you go."

After he said that I felt so much relief. He smirked down at me and backed away slowly. "Just know that if you run your mouth about anything, you'll end up like that woman's husband. Unlike his situation, your family won't have the fortune of ever finding your body."

WHAT WAS WRONG WITH ME?!

"BEFORE I GO, COME HERE." *He spoke in a very demanding voice.*

I GOT up and walked over to him. He grabbed my waist and pulled me closer to him. Our noses were barely an inch apart and he flashed a smile that made my heart melt. It felt like everything around us had stopped. One of his hands grabbed the back of my neck and he kissed me. He kissed me so hard that I stopped breathing. He pulled away and chuckled, licking his lips and walking out of the room in one swift movement. Hearing the lock on the door made me snap back into reality.

THIS WAS STRANGE.

"NOW YOU LISTEN TO ME, *and you listen closely." He spoke to me in a stern voice, asserting his dominance.*

MY EYES WIDENED as I nodded slowly. "O—Okay."

"NAH-UH." *He pulled my hands over my head and gripped both of my* wrists with one of his hands. "From now on you answer with 'yes sir,' Do I make myself clear?"

"Yes sir." I bit down on my lip and he smirked. He loved seeing me under his control. He wanted me to submit to him. He wanted to have complete dominance over me.

"Whatever I say, you do." He chuckled. "You didn't really think that tough girl act was going to cut it around me, did you?"

I opened my mouth to speak, but he cut me off. "Think before you answer, Lola."

"No, sir," I spoke quietly.

"Louder, Lola." He pushed himself closer to me.

"No, sir!!" I squealed, and the pace of my breathing increase.

"That's a really beautiful dress you're wearing, Lola." He spoke in a low tone, but loud enough for me to hear him. "Take it off."

He let go of my wrists and took a step back so that I could get undressed. I turned my back to him and slowly let down the zipper of my dress. I let the straps fall down my arms slowly and proceeded to pull it off of my chest. From where he was standing, it looked like a simple red bra, but then I turned around and the lace took him by surprise. He could see my breast through the thin material I had on.

I SLID the rest of my dress down to my ankles and kicked it across the room. I had on a matching pair of lace panties underneath of my fishnet stockings. I bet he thought it looked so beautiful laid across my long legs. He sat on the bed and just admired my body. Everything was happening in my favor and I couldn't be happier.

"TAKE off the stockings and bring them to me. When you make it over here, lay across my lap and do not make a sound," he said to me, and that's just what I did. Without hesitation, I complied with each demand and his expression showed that he loved every moment of it.

WHEN I MADE it over to the bed, I stood in front of him. I placed the stockings in his hand and laid across his lap. Laughing slightly under his breath, he pulled both of my hands behind my back and tied them together.

"GOOD GIRL," he spoke and I moaned slightly under my breath. He gave me a spank right on my ass and I squirmed in discomfort. "I thought I told you specifically to not make a sound, Lola. Don't make me punish you."

"YES, SIR," I whined and he gave me another spank.

"Don't say another word," Arsen instructed. He lifted my body and tossed me on the bed. He brushed my hair back out of my face to *admire my beauty. My skin was perfect and soft, and the color of lipstick I chose really made my eyes glow. I could tell by the way he looked at me. He looked me directly in the eyes and said, "You're never going home."*

I CLOSED my eyes and shook my head, trying to get rid of those thoughts. This wave of excitement had gotten really weird really fast. The first flashback hadn't been bad, but the other three referred to a couple of strange incidents that had happened between Arsen and I.

I PULLED myself out of my thoughts and saw that we were now parking in front of Arsen's home. I saw Ms. Rose standing at the door with a smile on her face and that made me ten times happier than before. I hadn't talked to her in a while—just small talk when she brought me my meals.

Arsen grabbed all of the bags and followed me inside of the house. Ms. Rose followed us upstairs as well. He dropped the bags off in my room and stood back to look at me. For a few seconds, we just stood there smiling at each other. He broke the awkwardness and gave me a hug.

"I HAD a great time with you today, Lola," he whispered in my ear. He gave me a soft kiss on the cheek and left my room, leaving me with Ms. Rose.

"HEY, DARLING. HOW WAS YOUR DAY?" She closed the door behind her and took a seat on my bed. She smiled as I sat down beside her.

. . .

"My day was great. Arsen took me out to get a new outfit for the interview that he got me." I smiled and began pulling out my items to show her.

"These are absolutely gorgeous." She ran her hand over the items of clothing and nodded her head. "You are going to look amazing in this."

"Wow! Thank you so much." This day had consisted of me smiling literally all day.
"He really likes you, you know." She put her hand on mine.

"Arsen?" I blushed. "I'm sure he does. Just not as much as I like him"

"I beg to differ." She let out a small laugh inside. "I heard your name multiple times before I even met you. You really are something special."

I looked down at my left hand, which was resting in my lap and tried to fight back yet another smile. That made me feel special. That definitely showed me that I was more important to him than I had actually thought I was. It made me feel warm inside.

. . .

"That makes me feel good." I directed my attention from my lap to Ms. Rose's face.

"As you should." She smiled and stood up from the bed. Without saying anything else, she left. As awkward as it sounded, it wasn't awkward at all. It felt really normal.

Not knowing what else to do, I decide to put my clothes away in the closet and lay in the bed. I laid on my back, pressing my head into the pillow. It was still the most comfortable bed I had ever slept on, especially compared to the ones that we sleep on in school.

I closed my eyes and imagined Arsen and I on a black sand beach. There was no one else on the entire beach but us. There was a big blanket laid out on the ground with various kinds of foods. We were having a picnic. I was wearing a long, flowy gown and Arsen was in a casual button up with shorts.

The weather was nice and so was the scenery. This was my dream date. We began making small talk and tasting the different food options that we had sitting around. He told me that there was something really important that he needed to tell me.

"Well, what is it?" I asked.

. . .

"I love you, Lola"

"You ...you love me?"
"Yes, Lola. I do"

I smiled, feeling at ease and content.

"I love you—"

"Lola!" I heard a voice yell in real life. I jumped up and it was Arsen. He was sitting on the edge of my bed. I guess I had drifted off to sleep and was actually dreaming instead of daydreaming.

"Sorry, I drifted off."

"Don't apologize. Sleep is natural. I'm not going to kill you or anything." We both looked at each other and laughed in unison. "I came to tell you about the job that you'll be doing for the cartel."

"Okay, tell me everything," I said sitting straight up.

"You're going to handle finances. This means we give you the money and you're responsible for putting it into our banks a little at a time so the bank doesn't get suspicious. Also, you manage our input and output online. You calculate exactly how much money we should be making and update us on if we are fulfilling that task. All right?"

"All right." I nodded. It seemed like a pretty easy job, especially for someone like me.

Arsen

After telling Lola exactly what she'd have to do for me, I went back in my room to tell the guys. I sent a simple text saying that she was working for us now. I didn't bother to call because I wanted to enjoy my day off instead of listening to them go on and on about what needed to be done. I could handle all of that when I was back on the job tomorrow.

Since Lola was now working for me, I had even more of a reason to keep her under lock and key. She was now a part of the gang, and since she was handling our money, her life was more in danger than ours. That's why I had asked her if she was sure. I knew she didn't like to be cooped up in that room for a very long time. We had to keep her safe and anonymous to the world if she wanted to handle a job like this.

There was a certain level of intelligence and power that you needed to be successful with this job. Lola had that, but was she ready to use it full force was the question. I heard a light tap on my door and I told whoever it was to come in. Lola walked in with a small smile on her face.

. . .

"Hey, Arsen. Um …you never locked my door."

"I know," I replied bluntly.

"Why is that?" she asked.

"You can walk around the house if you need to. Just learn how to mind your business." I laughed and she let out a small laugh as well. You could tell by the tone of her laughter that it kind of annoyed her, but it needed to be said.

"I actually wanted to know if we could watch movies together." She flashed a toothy grin.

"Right now?" I asked.

"Yeah." She looked over at the window, then back at me. "It's getting pretty dark outside and you didn't seem busy. I mean … unless you are busy. Then I'll totally just go back to my room."

"Uh, no. I'm not busy" I patted the space on the bed next to me. "Come sit. What kind of movie do you want to watch?"

. . .

"A French film," she blurted out loudly. She closed the bedroom door behind her before skipping over to the bed. She looked so cute in that silk shirt and short set that she used as pajamas.

"Any specific French film?" I laughed.

She nodded and slid the remote from out of my hand. She went directly to a movie about a younger girl and an older man. What a coincidence, huh?

I sat my back against the headboard and waited for the movie to start. Meanwhile, Lola was on the other side of me, tucking herself in under the blankets and cuddling up to my side. I chuckled at how adorable she was being and decided to get under the blankets as well. It was hot outside, but with the air on in the house, it often tended to be very cold.

I turned off my bed lamp. The only light would be from the sky and the TV. Her arms felt really warm wrapped around my waist. I liked this a lot.

About an hour into the movie, I felt her eyes staring at me. When I turn my head to look down at her, she kissed me. It wasn't just an innocent peck on the lips. It was full-force making out. It caught me by surprise, so for a couple of seconds, I just sat there, frozen. Then I realized I couldn't pass up this opportunity. So I put my hand on the back of her neck and began kissing back, deeply and passionately.

. . .

She pushed me on my back and rolled on top of me. I could feel her hands trying to pull my shirt off, so I took mine off and pulled hers off too. She wasn't wearing a bra, so she revealed her perfect breasts. I laid her on her back and hovered over her.

"Is this really what you want?" I asked. She nodded and pulled her bottom lip between her teeth.

I smirked and left a trail of kisses from the middle of her chest and up to her ear. I laughed softly and whispered in her ear. "I've been waiting so long to have you."

"Mmm." She let out a quiet moan. I lowered my head and let my mouth take turns licking and sucking over her nipples.
 Her head rolled back in slight pleasure, but this was only the beginning of it. I slid a hand into her shorts. She had on no panties. Good girl. I swirled my finger around between her folds and she moaned out in pure bliss.

I snatched her shorts off and licked my lips. I was going to make her submit to me. I stood up and slid my pants down, along with my boxers.

"Get on your knees, Lola," I demanded.

She got off of the bed and got on her knees before me. I

wrapped her ponytail around my hand and held her head back so that she was looking up at me.

"You're going to do whatever I say. Do I make myself clear?"

"Yes," she spoke, while licking over her lips.

"Yes, what?" I grinned evilly and pulled at her ponytail.

"Yes, sir!" She giggled.

24

LOLA

I never expected to be in this situation. Arsen was so frustrated that he *almost* wanted to skip the foreplay and just get straight to the sex. I took his shaft into my hand and jerked it slowly as I ran my tongue over the tip. I wanted to tease him. I kissed all around his member slowly, watching him grow bigger and harder.

I pushed him all the way into my mouth and began sucking him to the best of my abilities. We caught eye contact as I looked up at him and I began to deep throat him. His eyes slowly rolled to the back of his head as I throated him and massaged his balls with my right hand.

"Keep doing that," he groaned. "Ugh, you're such a good girl."

My heart nearly melted and I held him in my throat for a couple of seconds before gagging. He liked that a lot.

"All right, enough, enough. Get up."

"Yes, sir!" I replied and stood up, licking my lips.

"Hands and knees, now."

I nodded and crawled into bed, getting into the position that he had instructed. My first time being dominated in bed damn sure felt great.

He slapped my ass and pushed down on my neck. "Arch your fucking back, and you better keep it that way."

If I hadn't already been dripping wet, I was then. He was so aggressive and I loved every second of it. This was the sex I had dreamed of having since I first lost my virginity. Finally, something fun and exciting. I was tired of being the one who called the shots.

He had me on my hands and knees as he pleased me from behind. I had never felt more pleasured in my life before than in that moment. His strokes would constantly switch from being slow and sensual to being fast and rough.

No matter the pace he was going, it felt like heaven on earth. I wanted this feeling to last forever.

I screamed at the top of my lungs, so loudly that my moans were echoing off of the walls. I bit down on my lip to hold back the noise and felt myself getting close. Arsen had my face in the pillow and my hands behind my back.

His groans turned me on even more as he whispered sweet nothings into my ear. I finally came down from my high of sensual desires and fell onto the bed, breathless. He came moments later, onto my back.

"How was it?" I heard Arsen ask from over me.

"Amazing." I rolled on my back and smiled up at him. "You really do know how to make a woman feel amazing."

He placed a soft kiss on my lips and laughed. "I'm happy that I could make you feel on top of the world, baby girl."

He laid down next to me and I drifted off to sleep in his arms.

I woke up back in my bedroom. There were rose petals all over my bed and a note that said Arsen had had to leave early for work. I began to think back to when I first stayed the night.

"Lola, you don't have to hide from me. We're both old enough to be naked around each other and be comfortable with it." He walked by me and picked up my clothing from the floor. He placed them on a chair next to his desk and looked over at me again.

"Where will I be sleeping?" I tried changing the subject to take away from the awkwardness.

"With me, hopefully," he responded. "I respect whatever boundaries you have. I just haven't slept next to a beautiful woman in a long time."

I nodded slowly, not wanting to put up a fight, and climbed into bed. He turned off the light and got into bed next to me. Directly across the room was a huge floor-to-ceiling window and the curtains were pulled back completely. There was a beautiful view of not only the moon and stars, but over the city as well. I could see almost every building was well-lit and that alone made me feel safe. The light from outside made it easier to see around the room and to see that Arsen was staring at me staring at the view.

I looked over at him and smiled. "The view is beautiful. Thanks for letting me experience this"

"Anytime you want to see it, let me know" He ran his hand over my thigh and it drove me crazy. "You know, Lola, I've wanted you ever since I laid eyes on you"

"I'm well aware, Arsen," I replied bluntly, trying not to say too much.

"Well, do you feel the same way?" I felt him move a little closer to me.

"Maybe." I smirked and rolled over on my side. I felt him pull me back so that my body touched his and his hand grazed my leg.

"So why aren't we doing anything about that?" His hand slipped between my thighs and I began to melt, but I wasn't going to let him know that he had full control of my body at the moment. I pulled his hand away and laughed lightly.

"Goodnight, Arsen Lockhart."

"I really felt like the connection was there. I guess not," he spoke quietly. He moved back away from me and turned over. *"Whenever you're ready, Lola, just let me know."*

"Again," I smiled to myself. *"Goodnight, Arsen Lockhart,"*

Oh, how the times had changed. I went from trying to be uptight around him to making love in his California king bed. I felt truly refreshed.

The note also stated that Ms. Rose would be off for the next three days on vacation, so I could go downstairs and help myself to something to eat for breakfast. I slid out of bed, grabbed my robe, and headed downstairs to the kitchen. It was my first time ever being in there, so I was amazed at how big and nice it was.

I didn't really feel like cooking anything, so I looked around until I found a bowl and spoon to get some cereal. I sat at the island and ate in silence. I felt sort of out of place not eating a five-star breakfast in a huge bed, but I liked it. This way made me feel like I belonged here. I smiled and spun around on the stool.

"Hey, beautiful." I heard Arsen's voice and quickly snapped my head in his direction.

"Arsen!" I shouted excitedly and jumped down from the stool to run over to him. I wrapped my arms around his neck and gave him a big kiss.

"How are you?" He smiled and held my waist in his hands.

"I'm great." I smiled. "I thought you were at work"

"I came home for a quick lunch." He smiled and walked past me into the kitchen. He went in the fridge and pulled out a sandwich covered in plastic wrap. "Pre-made sandwiches are a blessing"

I laughed and grabbed my empty cereal bowl to put in the dishwasher. I looked over at Arsen, who had already started to eat his lunch. I picked up a napkin and wiped the side of his mouth. I just watched in amusement as he ate. I couldn't wait to see his reaction the day I cooked for him.

The next day Arsen taught me how to calculate how much money was supposed to be coming in and being sent out to the cartel's partners. It was pretty easy, like I expected. It just a process that took a lot of time and that you had to be very careful with.

After going through that mini-lesson, Arsen explained to me that I would be meeting the gang. I was extremely nervous for this. They all knew me as the nosey girl who had peaked through Arsen's email and put their cartel at risk.

The ride to the meeting was long and kind of boring due to not only the lack of conversation between Arsen and I, but also the lack of good music on the radio. We had to change the station at least three times. Nonetheless, I was very anxious, no matter how confident sitting in a car next to someone as beautiful as Arsen made me feel.

We finally made it to our destination and a took a deep breath. I looked in the mirror to make sure I looked presentable and just hoped for the best.

"Are you ready for this, Lola?" Arsen asked while watching me watch myself in the mirror.

"No, but I'll have to get it done whether I'm ready or not." I laughed a little.

"Then let's go, love." He got out of the car and started walking toward the building. I soon followed his actions and walked inside behind him.

He led me to a room in the back, where it smelled like beer and cigarettes. I hated the smell but I'd just have to deal with it.

"Guys, guys! Gather around!" Arsen called. He sat in a chair and pulled me onto his lap. All of the guys sat down in a group in front of us. "This is Lola and she'll be helping us out around here."

"What will she be doing, boss?" a random guy asked from the back of the group.

"I'll be handling all you guy's finances," I spoke up. "And trust me, you have nothing to worry about. I am completely trustworthy and a perfect fit for this job."

"Cool," the guy replied. "Welcome."

"Yeah, welcome" one of the men in the front spoke. The rest of the guys followed suit and welcomed me as well.

"Thanks, guys. I promise I won't disappoint." I smiled. Arsen then began telling me each of the member's names and their job, including their job outside of the cartel.

"Are you ready for your first task, Lo?" Arsen spoke in my ear and I agreed.

"We need you to take this money." Pete lifted a box up and sat it on the table separating them from Arsen and I.

"And put it into three different banks," David said sliding a piece of paper to me that had the bank's account number and information.

"Cool." I stood up and grabbed both the box and the piece of paper.

"I think you should wear three different outfits so no one will notice you going from bank to bank," Pete suggested.

"Actually," I stated. "If you guys have cards with these accounts, I can just go to the three different banks all over the town and maybe even go to one in the next city over."

"You got yourself a smart one, Lockhart," David chuckled which caused me to smirk.

"I know." Arsen laughed and slid his keys in my hand and a spare phone. "You can use my car, babe."

"Sweet," I replied and turned to him. "Thanks, babe!"

I leaned over and gave him a passionate kiss on the lips.

"Mmmm," I hummed as I pulled away and winked at him. "See you guys later."

"Geez, boss. How'd you pull one like that?" I heard one them mumble on my way out. I laughed at the comment and left the clubhouse.

When I got inside the car, I looked up the banks locations on the GPS and decided to go the ones that were all very far away from each other. Before I pulled off, I got a text from Arsen telling me to meet him back at his place when I was finished.

25

ARSEN

I texted Lola telling her to meet me at the house when she was done because David was going to give me a lift home.

"I see why you couldn't kill her," Pete laughed. "She's fucking gorgeous man. How'd you get her?"

I just raised an eyebrow in response.

"Not saying young, hot girls can't be interested in you," Pete said, holding his hands up in defense. "But that is a different level of hot, man. She's flawless."

"It just happened." I laughed. "I saw her and I knew I had to make her mine. I remember it like it was yesterday.

When I first laid eyes on her I knew she was the one. She had brown eyes, wavy hair, and plump lips painted a matte wine red. What first caught my eye was the smirk on her face when the teacher called out everyone's name and she didn't reply. As I watched her, I wondered how she could be bold enough to sit in on someone else's class.

I walked to the middle of the class with my hands behind my back to introduce myself and smiled. You could hear the silent whistles and occasional OMGs coming from the female students. All except for her. That was new for me. She didn't even move her eyes up from her bag to see what was going on. I was honestly caught off guard, being that I was always the center of everyone's attention when I walked into the room. A woman had never not taken an interest in me, so this random student not giving me the time of day made me drawn to her and only her. I loved a woman that I had to chase after a little.

So, of course, I started off my lecture with the basic, "Hello, ladies and gentlemen. My name is Arsen Lockhart and this is how I became a billionaire novelist." As soon as the word "novelist" slipped out, it was like something clicked inside of her brain. Her head popped up immediately and she began paying attention to everything I was saying.

We made eye contact from across the room, and from the moment I saw her, I knew I had to make her mine. She bit down on her lip as she watched me walk around the classroom. It was really a coincidence that on the day she had skipped her class, a great opportunity like this had come about. There had to be a reason the universe pulled us together.

I felt so deeply about her that telling the story to the guys made me fall for her all over again. Those almond shaped eyes and pouty lips made me weak, not to mention the sex we had. It was fucking amazing.

"Life just feels right with her in it." I smiled to myself.

"That's, uh, real beautiful, boss, but I just got an email that there's a new gang in town and they're trying to become the biggest gang here."

26

LOLA

Making the bank transactions was really easy, but while leaving the bank, I noticed that the crazy lady who had attacked Arsen on our first date was watching me from her car. The lady was oddly familiar. I drove past her slowly to try to remember exactly who she was.

THAT'S WHEN IT CLICKED! The crazy woman was Anabella's mom. She looked very sick and demented, which was probably why I didn't notice her in the first place. That explains why I saw her leaving my dorm building.

SHE STARED at me the entire time I drove past her and continued to watch until I was out of sight. It gave me goose bumps, honestly. The look on her face was terrifying. She looked dead inside.

. . .

I shook away the vision of her in my mind and just focused on getting back to Arsen. The drive back home was peaceful. I didn't bother to play the radio because I got lost in my writer's brain yet again.

If this were a scene in a book, the sky would be orange. No ... peach. The way it varied in three different shades would resemble the hombre of the juicy fruit. The clouds resembled the peach fuzz that grazes the thin layer of skin. The sun would be a yellow spot peeking through. Oh, what a beauty.

And what was I? Just an ant finding its way through the busy traffic of this hive we called life. The gush of wind was heavy, signs of a hurricane coming. Well ...a hurricane to an ant, that is.

Back in reality, it was just a simple summer's rain. And I was just a writer who was also a hopeless romantic when it came to Arsen Lockhart. For some reason, I always forgot that he was a murderer and a drug dealer. It was just that I never saw the bad side of him unless we were being intimate. It was scary to say, but even if I had seen that side of him, my feelings for him wouldn't have faded.

I called his phone twice, but there was no answer. The rain was pouring down. There was even a bit of thunder and lightning. When I opened the contacts application on the phone, I saw that the only other numbers were Ms. Rose and the driver. I didn't expect to find anything, but I opened the notes and there was actually something that I needed to see.

. . .

THE NOTE SAID that there was a spare key to the front door underneath the plant on the right-hand side of the front step. I got out and ran to the door to avoid getting wet. I got the key and opened the door. I didn't hear anything or see any sign of anyone being home. I shut the door behind me it and locked it.

I JOGGED upstairs to my room and got ready to take a shower. I had to wash this rain off of me. I tossed all of my clothes into the hamper and went into the bathroom. I ran the shower water until it got hot enough for my desires. I stepped inside and let the water kiss my skin.

THERE WAS nothing better than a hot shower after your first day on the job as a financier for a drug cartel. I kind of laughed to myself at the thought of the god-awful joke in my head. The shower was my favorite place to think. It gave me time to really process the things that were going on in my life. The number one thing that I was focused on processing at that moment was my relationship with Arsen.

WHERE DID our relationship go from here? Honestly. We had both shown each other how we feel, but neither of us has actually put it into words how we felt. It was strange. Two very bold and courageous writers, yet we both couldn't come up with the words to say to each other.

IT WAS CONFUSING, and honestly, I didn't think either of us had the answers to each other's questions at that very moment. But we both knew that we had strong feelings for each other. I think that we were both expecting and longing for that perfect speech in which we both expressed our undying love for each other. I didn't think that was going to come anytime soon.

So, we were just going to have to live in the moment. We just had to take a deep breath and exist as two human beings in like. My feelings for the man were going to be the death of me. I believed it more and more each day.

I COULD DEFINITELY SEE us spending our lives together in paradise. Just us two together, forming one bond. That was my dream life. That was the life I saw myself sharing with him. He was the perfect guy for me.

AS MUCH AS I loved to dig deep into my thoughts while taking a shower, it was time for it to come to an end. I washed my hair, face, and body until I was squeaky clean. When I got out, I headed directly toward my closet to find something to wear. I put on a sports bra and a pair of sweatpants. I put on a pair of slippers, too, because I wanted to go downstairs and find something to eat.

I MADE it downstairs to the kitchen to find something to eat. I didn't feel like cooking a full meal, so I pulled out whatever food was left in the fridge. I made a sub sandwich loaded with veggies and topped it off with a small amount of mustard and mayo.

AFTER EATING THE SANDWICH, I went right back to my room just to check on my schedule for tomorrow. The only thing that I had planned was to go grocery shopping and I was excited. I rolled over on my back and stared at the ceiling. Hopefully Arsen had enough free time to cook me something.

Like maybe we could go to the beach again or we could go dancing in a nightclub. Just something new. I had every right to be a dreamer and that's what I was doing. I was always daydreaming. My head was always in the clouds.

I just wanted to go out and spend time with him as much as I could. I knew that he was a very busy man and that being a billionaire didn't come easily, but I couldn't picture my day without him. I started to become really lonely without him around. I craved for his energy. I knew that I needed to be around him more than usual because our bond was starting to become unbreakable.

"Hey, baby girl." I heard his voice from the doorway and jumped up instantly.

"Hi!" I smiled. "I didn't know you were here."

"Yeah, I'm sorry about that. When I got home I decided to take a quick nap, but I think I fell asleep too deeply, as you can see." He shook his head. "I missed a lot of phone calls and texts."

. . .

He walked into the room and came and sat down next to me. He used his index finger and thumb to brush my hair back behind my ear. Such an innocent gesture, but it held so much passion within it. I leaned in and left a peck on his lips. This wasn't love, but it was something very close to it.

27

ARSEN

We both woke up in Lola's bed. My arms were wrapped around her and her head was laying on my chest. This was a moment of pure bliss.

"Good morning," I whispered as I placed a kiss on her forehead.

"Morning." She yawned and sat up.

"Let's go get some breakfast." I stood up from the bed scooped her up into my arms. I carried her all the way downstairs to the kitchen and sat her down on the counter.

"Pancakes, please," she uttered in a soft tone.

"Pancakes it is, sweetheart." I smiled and proceeded to take out all of the ingredients that I needed.

I turned on the radio and opened up the curtains to the kitchen's patio. When she laid eyes on the backyard, so much excitement grew within her.

"You have a pool and didn't tell me??" She hopped off of the counter and ran over to the patio door. She unlocked it and went outside to look around.

I laughed at her excitement and pulled a packet of maple bacon out of the freezer. Ms. Rose told me about how she loved this kind of bacon the most. I sat some out on a pan and put it in the oven. While I waited for them to cook, I began making my special apple cinnamon pancakes.

She'd never had my cooking before, so I wondered how she'd react. She came back in and walked over to me.

"Can I make coffee, babe?" She looked up at me. "And your backyard is stunning, if I may say so myself."

"Thanks." I chuckled. "And of course you can make coffee. The machine is over there. Make a big pot for the both of us."

"Got ya.'" She nodded and started to make the coffee.

The only sounds that were audible at that moment were the sizzling of the bacon in the oven, the coffee brewing, and the soft music coming from the radio. I finished up the pancakes and put some on plates for the both of us.

I took the bacon out of the oven and I heard Lola gasp. I couldn't help but burst out into laughter. Everything was just so exciting to her today.

"Is that the maple kind?!" she asked.

"Yes." I laughed out loud and shook my head. "Ms. Rose told me all about how you loved it, so I had to make it."

"I love her. She's so sweet." Lola smiled and poured some of the fresh pot of coffee into two cups for us. I watched as she put an equal amount of sugar and cream into her coffee. "Sugar and cream?"

"Um, just about two tablespoons of sugar," I told her. "I like mine mostly black. For more energy and just a little sugar for flavor."

"I don't know how you do it," she laughed. "It just tastes too bitter to me without any cream"

"I used to feel that way about it, too, but it eventually grew on me." I smiled and put the cooled-down bacon on our plates. I grabbed us a few utensils and the bottle of syrup and sat it up to look nice.

I quickly cut up a couple of fresh fruits and laid them over the pancakes. "Breakfast is complete"

Lola walked over to me with the two cups and placed one in front of each plate. I smiled at the sight and sat down to begin eating. Lola did the same.

"Mmm," I heard her moan as she took a bite of the pancakes. "They're so fully and the apples just melt in your mouth."

I smirked. "Yeah, I'm pretty talented in the kitchen."

"You're talented everywhere, Arsen," she giggled.

"Well ...yeah, you're right." We both looked at each other and laughed.

When we were both finished, we headed back upstairs to get ready for our day. I was going to the clubhouse to talk business with the boys today, but since we had awoken early, I actually had time to go grocery shopping with Lola.

We parted ways after going back upstairs, for the sake of being able to spend more time with each other. We both took quick showers and got dressed in our rooms.

I walked back in Lola's room and watched as she put on very natural-looking makeup. "Hey, Lo, do you think you can check the bank to see if all of our money secure?"

"Of course, babe," she said, getting up and walking over to the computer. She put in all of the information carefully and read over the details. "Okay, bae, everything looks pretty fine now. It just says that someone took out $40."

"That's strange." I raised an eyebrow. "Maybe one of the guys needed cash really quick. I'll ask when I meet up with them later on."

She nodded and logged out of everything, making sure to not leave anything open. I taught her well.

"Ready?" I asked.

"Yup!" She got up and wrapped her arms around my neck. She kissed me deeply and I kissed back, biting at her bottom lip.

"You're going to get yourself in trouble kissing me like that." I smirked.

"I like trouble." She smiled and turned to leave the house. I smacked her ass and she squealed. It was the cutest thing ever. I followed her downstairs and outside to the driveway.

"You can drive." I tossed her the keys. "We're taking the corvette."

"Sweet!" she yelled out and got into the front seat. I got in on the passenger side and we were off.

She turned on the music and blasted it. They were playing all of the best classical rock songs again, so we had to sing along at the top of our lungs. The morning air felt absolutely amazing against my skin and I felt like I was on top of the world. All because I was spending time with the girl of my dreams.

Life was going great. When we pulled up to the grocery store, Lola found the perfect parking space right out front. We got out and went inside. I opened the list and we took our time walking around to get the items that we needed.

Once we got everything that we needed, I paid and we left. That had gone faster than I expected and it made me kind of sad that we would be parting ways soon.

"Hey, babe?"

"Yes, my love?" she answered me.

"Do you want to go with me to meet up with the guys?" I looked over at her as we pulled up to a red light.

"Of course." She smiled.

"All right." I smiled. "We can go there now. Do you remember how to get there?"

"Yup." She put emphasis on the 'p' and sped off as soon as the light turned green.

Nearly a half an hour later, we were finally pulling up to the clubhouse. I saw all of the other cars, so like the usual, everyone was there waiting for me.

I walked in with Lola and everyone exchanged greetings.

"So, what's new?" I asked, sitting down and pulling Lola down on my lap.

"Nothing much. Everything is pretty much going great," David spoke up.

"Great," I said. "Oh, whoever took $40 out of the bank yesterday, we need you to put it back because it wasn't time to distribute money yet."

All the guys looked around at each other confused.

"No offense, Arsen, but none of us took any money out of the bank," Pete spoke.

I grabbed the laptop on the table and opened it. "Babe, show them," I whispered in Lola's ear.

She entered all of the information carefully and suddenly she felt tense.

"What the fuck!" she yelled, while dropping the laptop on the table.

"What is it?!" I sat up in my seat.

"Someone stole $20,000 dollars from the accounts all together! The transactions just happened about 15 minutes ago!"

The room became loud. All of the boys were yelling about what was going on and I was absolutely furious.

"Go take the groceries home," I said to Lola calmly. I walked her to the front door and kissed her on the forehead. "We have some business to take care of."

"You sure you don't need me here, babe?" she asked. She was pleading with me to be allowed to stay with the look in her eyes.

"Just go, baby." I sighed and kissed her. "I'll see you when I get home. I love you."

28

LOLA

"I—I love you too" I smiled and left out of the clubhouse. I was completely disturbed by the fact that someone was stealing money from Arsen, but the way he kissed me and told me he loved me made me feel like I was floating on a cloud.

I GOT in the car and began to drive back to Arsen's house. I wondered if it was something that I had done, or if it had something to do with Anabella's mom, because of the way that she had been watching me when I left the bank. I picked up the spare phone that Arsen gave to me and texted him that the crazy lady who had attacked him the night of our first date was Anabella's mother and she was watching me as I left the last bank. The look on her face had been so sinister. She looked as if she had just escaped a mental asylum.

I DECIDED to just listen to some classical music to calm my nerves on the way back home, because just the thought of seeing Anabella's mother that way sent chills up my spine. I heard a pop and the car began to slow down. Great, a flat tire is exactly what I needed right now. I sighed deeply and got out of the car to see exactly which tire it was. I went around to the side of the car and saw that it was the front. right tire.

I HEARD the sound of a car pulling up behind my car and stopping. Then a man walked up behind me and asked if I needed any help. Me being the skeptic that I was, I lied and said that I'd be all right and that I had already called the police and my boyfriend. They were both nearby and would be here in no time. Just when I thought he had actually walked away, he hadn't.

I FELT a piece of cloth covering my mouth and my body being jerked back into somebody else's. I tried to scream at the top of my lungs, thinking that someone would hear being that it was broad daylight. But there was no one around. They picked me up and threw me in the back of a car. The cloth was now tied around the back of my head so that I couldn't make a sound. Tears streamed down my face because I felt so hopeless.

WHY WAS this happening to me?

I MANAGED to push the cloth out of my mouth and yelled for help as loudly as I could. Something hit me over the head and everything started going to black.

29

ARSEN

I got a text from Lola saying that she saw Anabella's mom watching her at the bank when she went to deposit the money. That gave us a major lead in finding out who exactly stole the money. We had this new gang in town who wanted to say they were the biggest and the best around town, but to become that they would have to take us down, because that's our spot. Anabella and her mom were both out to get us because of the deaths of their horrible husband/father. There were two groups of people out to get us and either they were just trying to get what they wanted individually or they were working together.

I was sick of trying to play nice when it came to these people who threatened my life and played with my money. I didn't take kindly to threats. If you threatened me or ruined any source of my income, you would lose your life.

"Donnie, get their information now! We're ending this tonight," I screamed angrily.

"What do you want us to do, boss?" One of the members, Jacob, asked me.

"What do you think? Start loading the guns and packing

them up. We're going on a man hunt tonight, and we won't rest until we find who stole from us"

"Got ya, boss!" Jacob nodded and went into the back with a couple of guys.

"Pete, take the others to go fill up the trucks with gas," I instructed. "David, you stay with me"

"Sure thing, boss," Pete said. The rest of the members followed him out of the back door.

"David, why do people keep trying to mess with us? All we ask is that people stay out of our way and we'll stay out of theirs, but some people are too dumb to even respect that. So, they deserve to lose their life." I started to pace around.

"I'm not sure, but what I do know is that they've messed with the wrong team and everyone can use this as an example of what not to do when it comes to messing with us," David responded.

I picked up a glass and threw it against the wall. That's how frustrated I was. Hearing the glass shatter as it broke sort of calmed me down. It made me think clearly again. If we were going to take down the enemy, we would have to be calm, but also have an amazing plan. Rule #1 of our personal cartel business was to never let the enemy get away with anything.

30

LOLA

I woke up in the back seat of a car, my hands attached to my head from the heavy pounding. My wrists were tied together and so were my ankles. I fully opened my eyes to see some random man driving at a slow pace. His face was very emotionless in the rear-view mirror and his hand was gripping the steering wheel a little too tightly.

"WHY AM I IN HERE?" I asked quietly. He paid no attention. He kept his eyes on the empty road ahead. "WHY?!" I yelled.

"WILL YOU SHUT THE FUCK UP?" He screamed, gripping the steering wheel tighter than before. "God, you dumb *bitch*! You just woke up and the first thing you do is talk"

"WELL, what do you expect me to do when I've been kidnapped?" I mumbled, rolling my eyes. "Who the hell are you and why are you kidnapping me?!"

. . .

"Shut ...up." His voice was very stern and demanding. Intimidating as well.

The car came to an abrupt stop and the next thing I knew, I was being snatched out of the car by multiple people and being dragged into some random house.

I wasn't sure where I was, but I didn't like it. I wasn't safe there and all I wanted was just to be with Arsen. Whoever had kidnapped me brought me to a house, walked me upstairs, and made me sit in a room that had nothing but a rollaway bed and a window. It was cold and had very little light. I think it may have been the attic.

What did I ever do to deserve this?

31

ARSEN

It was finally dark outside, so the plan was in full effect. My guys tracked down the new gang's clubhouse. We also found out the computer that was used to steal money from our banks had an IP address that linked back to that same clubhouse address. Not only was that new gang the one stealing from us, that house that they had their clubhouse meetings in was in fact Anabella's mother's house. Anabella and her mother must have called in for backup when they realized I wasn't afraid of them.

It took two trucks to fit all of us. We drove about five to ten minutes away from one another, so no one would be too suspicious. When we all arrived, we huddled. There was going to be a group of people going through the front door and another going through the back. We all drew our guns and got of the trucks. The group in the backyard had gone around to the back door already. My group was now approaching the front door.

"One ... two ... three ..." I yelled and kicked the door in. We all ran in with our guns and demanded that everyone got on the ground. We went all around the house, rounding everybody up downstairs. Once we all had them backed into a corner, we all smiled.

"Hi, Anabella." I chuckled as she tried to hide behind the others. "Bye, Anabella."

Everyone just started shooting at the crowd of people and we didn't stop until each and every one of them were dead. I shook my head at the gruesome scene and ordered for everyone to start collecting the drugs and money.

After we collected all of their things, we ran out back toward the trucks. Just as we were driving away, Anabella's mother appeared on the scene. I shot at her through the window, but didn't look back to see whether I had killed her or not.

We got back to the clubhouse to discard all of the clothes we were wearing and to clean the guns. After everyone had cleaned up and changed, we opened the bags to see exactly how much we had gotten from them. I gave David the pleasure of counting the money and Pete the honor of seeing how many drugs we took.

"They had exactly fifty-five thousand dollars sitting around like it was nothing," David said and all of the guys cheered. It always felt amazing coming into a shitload of money.

"We managed to get four bricks of cocaine, as well," Pete said and the guys cheered once again. This was amazing.

My phone began to ring and the room got really quiet. I let it ring two more times and finally answered.

"Hello?" I asked.

"Yes, is this Mr. Arsen Lockhart?" a man answered on the other end.

"This is him," I replied bluntly.

"Hi, this is detective John Downey from the city's police department. We found a corvette registered under your name completely empty on the side of the road."

"WHAT?!" I questioned.

"Yes, sir. Is this your car? It had a flat tire and the driver's door was slightly left open," the detective said and my heart dropped.

"My ...my girlfriend was driving it. Are you sure you guys didn't see her?"

"No, sir. The car was completely empty. Your girlfriend is missing." I dropped the phone from my ear and stood there in complete shock.

A BILLIONAIRE'S FATE

An Alpha Billionaire Romance

By Michelle Love

32

LOLA

Three men barged into the room and closed and locked the door behind them. Frightened, I pushed myself into the corner of the bed as best as possible and watched them closely. Just then I heard multiple gunshots coming from downstairs and a lot of footsteps running around. I screamed at the loud sound and was instantly punched in the face by one of the men.

I gasped, completely shocked and in pain. I kicked my feet at him, despite my ankles being tied together, and hit him on the side. I immediately regretted the decision when I felt multiple blows to the face. The pain was crazy and I tasted blood spilling from my lip. I knew better than that the next time.

All the while, there were still multiple shots going on downstairs. I couldn't tell if people were shooting at the house or if the people in the house were shooting at someone else. I was hoping someone would kick down the door and get me out.

It seemed like it took hours for the shooting to stop, when it was really just a couple of seconds. I squirmed in the bed and laid on my bed, sobbing softly. I made sure to keep an eye on all of the men while doing so.

"What are they doing?" The man who hit me asked the man listening through the door.

"Sounds like they're taking all of our stuff!"

"Shit!" The third one yelled in a whisper.

"I'd stop them, but it's too many to take on. It's a guarantee that we'd get shot in an instant" The man by door whispered and shook his head.

By the way they were talking, I could tell the others were against them. I wondered if they could potentially save me, but I was terrified and not in the mood to be beaten in the face again. Who knew? I could scream and they could put a bullet right through my brain.

33

ARSEN

"What's wrong, boss?!" David asked, running over to me and picking up the phone.

"Lola." I just stood there, staring into space. I was still trying to wrap my mind around the concept of Lola actually being gone.

"What about her?" Pete asked.

"She's gone."

"Gone?" David took a step closer. "What exactly do you mean by 'gone,' Arsen?"

"Gone!" I yelled. "Someone kidnapped her from the side of the road. The detective said something about a flat tire."

The room fell silent and the air grew thick around us. It was as if no one knew what to do or what to say, and I understood completely. I looked around the room and saw that everyone else was sitting down. I couldn't wrap my mind around the thought that she was gone just that fast.

"I'm going to go find her." I grabbed my jacket from the coat hanger and threw it on.

"Boss, it's eleven o'clock. You should really get some rest and look for her in the morning," Pete suggested.

"You must be out of your mind to believe that I'm just going to leave her out there alone and in danger." I scoffed.

"You don't even know where to start looking, Arsen. Let's be real here." David spoke, standing up from his seat and walking over to me. Pete followed shortly behind him.

"What if your wife was missing? You would lose your mind. You'd search all over the world for her the minute you found out, David. You too, Pete. So don't even act like you don't understand where I'm coming from." I forced out a stiff laugh and looked over at David. "Give me a ride home, will ya?"

"All right, man. Whatever." He grabbed his keys and threw on his jacket. I walked out of the building to his car and he soon followed behind me.

We got in the car and headed off to my place. There was so much running through my mind. I didn't even know if she were dead or not, and that's what troubled me the most.

We finally made it back to my place and I went inside without saying any goodbyes to David. I walked straight up to Lola's room to see if she was there. I knew she wasn't there, but I felt like I had to do it. Her room was completely empty and really cold. It was as if the house could tell she was missing too. I hated it.

It was usually cool in her room, but her spirit and presence gave off a peculiar warmth. I got a dizzy feeling, but quickly shook it off and walked down to my room. I plopped my body down on the bed and rolled over onto my back. I sort of felt myself falling asleep until I was interrupted by my phone ringing. It was a blocked number.

"Hello?" I answered quickly.

"Arsen?" I heard a small woman's voice.

"Lola?!" I asked, now sitting up on my bed.

"Help me," she mumbled out.

"Lola, baby. Where are you?!" I asked frantically.

"She's with me," I heard a male voice speak up.

"And who the fuck are you?!"

"Don't worry about that. You could've had your precious Lola if you had looked in the attic of the house you shot up." He chuckled. "But don't worry now. We're not there anymore"

"I'll find you and I'm going to kill you," I spoke quietly.

"You want the girl back? Fifty thousand dollars. I want everything you stole from us back."

"Fine," I agreed. "Where are you going to meet me?"

"I'll let you know soon. If you fuck this up, I'm going to kill the girl"

"I'll kill your entire family with no remorse," I spoke calmly, trying to now show him how angry I was. "I will leave you deserted with not even a dime to your name. Do you really want that?"

He scoffed. "I'll tell you when and where to meet me."

The phone clicked, indicating that he hung up, and I dropped it on the bed. I slammed my fists down on the red sheets, then ran a hand through my hair. I couldn't believe that I had let them touch her like that. I was so stupid and careless, letting her go home by herself. Especially after she told me that Anabella's mom was watching her like some kind of creep.

I stood there, not really knowing what to do. I was going out of my mind and wasn't sure how to get over it. I breathed deeply and decided to take a shower. I didn't know how I would able to sleep, knowing that my princess wasn't in the other room safe and sound.

34

LOLA

I was being carried out of the house that I had been locked in earlier. There was a heavy smell of rotting flesh in the air. When I dared to open my eyes while passing by the living room, I caught a glimpse of Anabella. She was dead. I had never felt sicker to my stomach. My best friend since forever was dead and I wasn't sure how to deal with myself. She was lying in the arms of her mother, who caught me staring and came charging toward me as I was being carried to the car.

When I was placed into the back seat, her mother pushed the man out of the way and gave me a horrible slap across my cheek with the back of her hand. Her sharp ring left a gash on my cheek.

"What the fuck was that for?!" I screamed, while attempting to kick my feet. The restraints on my wrists and ankles made it impossible for me to defend myself.

. . .

"This is all your fault, you bitch!" She slapped me again. I couldn't believe this was happening.

"What did I even do?!?!" I screamed.

"You let that killer into your life, you traitor!" She screamed in my face.

My eyebrows knitted together as my face cringed. Was she talking about Arsen? Then it snapped in my head. She screamed that Arsen had killed her husband, which would be no one else but Anabella's dad. I stared blankly at her as flashbacks started to play in my head.

It was just two years ago. It was summer and Anabella and I were getting ready to go to the beach. She stepped out into the hall to take a call and ran back into the room minutes later, screaming and crying. It was the most horrible thing I'd ever seen and all I could do was hold her while she cried.

When she finally calmed down, I got her to talk to me.

"You remember when I told you my dad worked for a drug cartel?" She asked, looking up at me.

"Yes," I nodded. "What happened, Ana?"

"They killed him!!! They're trying to say he betrayed them, but I know my dad would never do that!" She cried even harder.

. . .

"OH MY GOD." My heart dropped. "I am so very sorry, Ana. I'm so sorry that you have to go through this."

"ALL OF THOSE fuckers are extremely rich, so if he did any of the things they claimed he did, it's not like they would be losing any money." She held me closer. The only thing I felt as if I could do was stay quiet and listen. She needed to get all of her emotions out.

"WHY COULDN'T they have just fired him?! Why did they have to take my father's life away?! He had a family that he loved so much and we loved him!" She was crying uncontrollably and I felt horrible. I hated whoever did this to her and her family.

HER DAD WAS ALWAYS SO nice and sweet to me. After his death, I had never seen Anabella's mother again. She was always locked away in her room when I went over and never cared about what Ana or her siblings were doing. I guess his death had made her terribly sick, because she wasn't as beautiful and radiant as she used to be. She looked sick and evil, which made it hard for me to even recognize her at the restaurant.

I SHOOK my head slowly as she screamed and yelled at me. Her words were going in one end and out of the other. All I could think about was why Arsen had done that. Was I being used by him to antagonize their family? I hoped not. I didn't want to speak to him, but at the same time I just wanted to be safe in his arms.

• • •

Did Arsen kill Anabella? Was I next to die?

All of those questions were weighing heavily on my mind. I wasn't sure if I could take it. I got really dizzy and everything around me was spinning. I heard the back door close and I drifted away into pure darkness.

I woke up in a different house. I was tied to a chair and my head was still spinning.

"We're going to make a call to your little friend, Lola! Are you ready?" I heard a male's voice.

I tried opening my eyes, but they felt swollen. I could only see slightly between my eyelashes. I saw Ana's mom and three other men standing across the dimly lit room, watching me. There was one guy kneeled in front of me with a phone in his hand.

"I said are you fucking ready?!" I felt a hard smack against my face and I winced. The stinging sensation was almost unbearable, but my vocal cords weren't letting me muster up a scream.

I nodded my head slowly and it felt like I was going to pass out again. I'd probably die if I didn't have a glass of water soon.

• • •

"Hello?" I heard Arsen's voice and that made me stronger in a sense. I felt like I could hold on a bit longer.

"Arsen?" I called out for him. I couldn't speak very loudly, but I tried for him.

"Lola?!" He asked. His voice was so loud that I couldn't tell if he was on the phone or in the room. My eyes were now completely shut.

"Help me," I mumbled out, not being able to say much else.

"Lola, baby. Where are you?!" That was the last thing I heard before my mouth was covered with a cloth with a very distinct smell.

As soon as I inhaled it, I began to choke, and soon felt myself fading into the darkness again.

35

ARSEN

I tossed and turned all night. There wasn't much I could do but wait for that call to say that I could get my Lola back. I got dressed and looked into the mirror. Bags were starting to form under my eyes and my hair was out of place. I pulled a comb through my hair and left the bathroom.

I grabbed a bottle of water on my way out of the house and hopped outside of my car. I was going to meet up with the boys for breakfast and explain everything that was going on.

I was too afraid to turn on any music, thinking that it would only remind me of the times that I had shared with Lola. The only thing on my mind was getting her back. All I wanted was her and I'd do anything to have her. She was the light to my darkness and the stars to my night sky, and that was something that I couldn't give up.

I pulled up to the restaurant and parked on the side of the building. I walked inside and was immediately escorted to the back room where all of my friends were sitting and waiting for me. They sat us down and sent a waitress into the room to take our drink order. It was early in the day, but some of the guys insisted on getting a beer while the rest of us settled for coffee.

"Guys, I brought us here all today to tell you guys the good and bad news."

"What is it?" one of the guys asked from the other end of the table.

"The good news is that the kidnappers are willing to give Lola back."

"And the bad news?" David looked at me.

The waitresses came back with our drinks and I got silent. They didn't need to know our business. They took our food orders and walked back out.

"Anyways," I sighed. "They want everything we stole back. Meaning the entire fifty thousand, even though they stole a majority of that from us"

The guys threw up their hands in disappointment and all groaned in agony. No one seemed willing to give up the money, which was why I had thought of a plan while I was in the shower that morning.

The room fell quiet again as the waitresses came back into the room with our food. They had weird looks on their faces because of how immediately quiet it had become. They sat our plates in front of us and left us alone once again.

"So, what's the plan?" David asked, noticing the look on my face.

"I want you guys to hide out, and when it's time for us to exchange, take them out. All of them. And we leave with both the money and Lola." I took a sip from my cup of coffee. The warmth of the cup laid upon the pads of my fingers.

"That's a damn good idea," Pete said, laughing and picking up a piece of bacon.

I flashed a slight smile and nodded.

"I'm down," David chuckled.

The rest of the members agreed and began eating their breakfast. I, on the other hand, wasn't eating, because I hadn't ordered anything. I knew I couldn't keep any food down with the thought of some asshole's hands all over her body. I cringed and finished my drink.

I got a call from a blocked number again and answered it instantly.

"Hello?" I answered,

"This bitch is fucking annoying," he spat from the other line.

"*Excuse me?*" I asked with a bit of attitude.

"She has a big mouth. Doesn't know when to shut the fuck up," He chuckled.

"You little—" I started but was cut off.

"650 Promise street. Tonight at twelve," he said, then hung up the phone.

When I sat the phone down, all of the guys were staring at me.

"Looks like we have a mission tonight, boys. 650 Promise Street. Tonight at twelve sharp," I sighed. I was frustrated at how he had talked about her, but I was happy that I got to get her back into my arms.

The boys all cheered and laughed, surprisingly. I thought they'd be bummed that they'd have to set this all up on short notice, but I guessed the rush of doing this and keeping the money filled them with excitement.

"Meet me at the clubhouse at nine to prepare," I said, while standing. I dropped just enough money to pay for everyone's meal on the table and left. All I could think about was seeing Lola's beautiful face again.

36
LOLA

I had been tied down to this chair since we got here, and I couldn't feel my body. I didn't think I had the ability to feel anything anymore. My face was swollen terribly, my wrists felt as if they were going to break, my hair was dirty, and my clothes had accumulated all of the dust that filled this dirty room.

I was starving—starving and nearly dehydrated. I found myself praying to god and asking why was this was happening to me. Although I'd never been friendly, I wasn't mean either. I was just always focused on myself. Was this what I got for worrying about myself? Or was this what I got for hanging out a drug-dealing billionaire?

The possibilities were endless, but I knew in that very moment that I didn't care about what Arsen had done. I was still very hurt about what he had done to Anabella's father and the possibility that he may have killed her, too, but all I wanted was to be in his arms.

The way things were going, I thought I would never see him again. Not him, not my family, and not even my best friend. I so felt completely helpless and hopeless, but if I had died right then, I couldn't care less. I guessed this was what I had signed up for when I fell in love with Arsen in the first place.

How wonderful life would have been right now if I hadn't skipped class to be with my best friend. She would have still been alive and we could have been having so much fun over the summer break. I would have never met him and I would have never fallen in love, but then again, I would have never remembered those moments of being young again. I would have never fallen in love. Who knew there could be two sides developing feelings for someone?

That feeling that went way beyond being friends or considering each other as family. The feeling of pure bliss and serenity while being around that one person. Being around someone who could bring back memories that you wished you could relive or create moments that you wished would never end. That's what I felt with him. Not with any of my ex-boyfriends, not with my family, and not even with my own best friend. I had known my relationship with Anabella was going to come to an end soon, but I had never thought it would end with her being dead.

This was not what I wanted. I never wanted her to be in pain, I never wanted to betray her, I never wanted to fall in love, and I never even wanted to meet someone new. I had thought my past would just stay in the past, but when it was brought back up, it felt so good that I couldn't deny it. I couldn't push it away. It had come alive in my mind and it was here to stay.

I had gotten so caught up in my love for a man who I barely knew that I was ignoring my best friend's cry for help. Although she had refused to tell me what was wrong when I was genuinely confused, I still felt like I could have tried a little harder to find out. It was too late now. She was gone and I didn't think I'd ever be able to see Arsen again.

I was sitting there, trapped in a room, practically losing my mind and giving up on life. It had only been two days, but my life had changed drastically. My mindset was completely different from how it was before. If I made it out of there alive, I was going to live with no regrets and I was going to treat every day like it was my last. But, then again, who knew?

This day might really be my last day.

I felt the tears begin to fall down my face. The things that were going through my mind were sickening. My breath began to quiver and I became nauseous. The pain that was buried inside of me at that moment was unbearable. Death seemed like the only way out.

37

ARSEN

When I got home, I changed into my sweats and decided to take a short nap. I knew that it would be hard for me to sleep because the thought of Lola was on my mind heavily, but I thought that the reassurance that I would have her back in my arms in just a couple of hours would help me rest a little bit. I closed my eyes and began to drift off.

"I love you with all of my heart, Arsen. You're the best thing that has ever happened to me," Lola said, stroking my hair gently.

She used her free hand to caress the side of my face. Her eyes stared deeply into mine and I felt my heart beat so fast that it began to melt. As painful as that sounds, it felt so good. It felt so right. Like we were meant to be here together, with one another. It felt as if we were already a couple. Like we had already made it official. Like we had already broadcasted it to the world.

. . .

I turned away from her for a quick second to admire the view of the sunset behind us. It was breathtaking. Truly stunning. But it wasn't as beautiful as her.

When I turned back to look at her, she was gone. The sky had instantly turned black and all I could hear were her screams in the distance. We were no longer on the beautiful and dreamy island. There wasn't even a "we" anymore. It was just me, standing in nothing but darkness. Pitch blackness surrounded me and engulfed me in its terror. I didn't know where to run or which way to turn, but I knew that I had to find Lola. And I had to save her.

"Man, get up." I heard David speak outside of my dream, waking me up.

I gave him a confused look, wondering what he was doing here and how he even got inside.

"Rose," was all he said, answering the questions that I hadn't yet gotten the chance to ask. I nodded in response and sat up on the bed. I ran both hands on my face and then through my hair.
"What is it? What's the problem?" I asked.

"It is 9:15, man. How long have you been asleep?" he asked, and my eyes widened.

. . .

"Honestly, it felt like only a couple of minutes, but I guess in actuality it was a couple of hours."

"Get dressed, boss. It's time to go get your girl back." He smirked and left the room.

I got dressed in my all-black outfit. It was go time and I felt stronger than I was before. I was on a mission to get Lola back and that was just what I was going to do. I had made a promise to myself that I would keep her safe and under my watch at all times, but I failed and it was time for me to redeem myself.

I got my phone off the nightstand and headed out to get inside of the car with David. We sped off into the night, driving as fast as we could to make it to the clubhouse. It was time to prepare and get ready for everything that was coming for us. I had a strong feeling that they were going to try to pull some type of trick on us and try to kill us. We weren't going to let that happen.

When we pulled up to the clubhouse, we quickly hopped out and went inside. The rest of the guys were dressed in their all-black outfits and waiting for us. The bags were packed and loaded with guns. There was one specific bag for me that sat on the table. It was the bag that we were supposedly going to exchange for Lola.

I grabbed the box of gloves and handed them to everyone. They knew what time it was. We packed our things inside of the truck and were on our way. The street they wanted to meet us on was in the next town over, so we had to leave a bit early to make it there just in time for us to set up. The guys held great conversations with each other on the ride there. The funny part about it was that none of the conversations contained worry about what was about to happen in an hour.

When we made it to the street, we parked in the far corner. We left one person in each truck to sit behind the steering wheel for when the job was done. I stayed in the car with the bag so that I could see when the scumbag pulled up with Lola.

The other members checked their surroundings and made their way over to the buildings, where they cut the connections to the keys of these specific buildings so that they could make it up to the roof. When they made it up there, they laid down and hid so that no one could see them. By then, I was getting anxious. I hadn't seen her face in two whole days and I was hoping that it looked exactly the same, or things might not get too pretty.

When I saw the car arriving, I placed a gun into the back of my pants and hid it beneath my jacket. It was a little cool out that night. I grabbed the bag and proceeded to walk toward their car. I stopped in the middle of the street and waited for them. When the driver's door opened, only one man got out, but I wasn't dumb enough to believe that he was alone.

He walked around to the back door of the car on the right side and opened the door. He grabbed a girl by the arm and pulled her out. But that wasn't my Lola. It couldn't have been. Her face was swollen and badly bruised. He had to hold her up because her legs looked extremely weak and she looked extremely pale and lifeless. Her hair was a mess and all over the place. This looked nothing like Lola.

"This isn't her," I said and a smile crept on his face.

"It's me, Arsen." I heard her speak. It was very low, but I knew it was her and my heart broke. I could feel the tears begin to swell in my eyes, but I fought them back.

"Give her to me," I demanded.

"Not just yet," he said. The smirk on his face was the most horrendous thing I had ever seen. "Give me the money and I'll give you the girl. It's a part of our deal."

I threw the bag of money toward him. When I went to go grab Lola, his gang came from around each corner, pointing their guns at me. There were about three on each side, which made it easy for my men to take them out.

"Do you really want to do this?" I questioned, while raising an eyebrow. A smile appeared on my face and I cleared my throat.

Just then, bullets rained down from the building tops, hitting each and every member, except for the man holding Lola. I pulled out my gun and aimed it directly toward him. I moved it over just a little and pulled the trigger. The bullet hit Anabella's mother directly between the eyes, killing her instantly. She thought I hadn't seen her, but I watched her as she looked through the window of the car the entire time.

THE GUY DROPPED Lola onto the ground and tried to make a run for it. I allowed him to make it all the way to the car before shooting him in the back of the head. He died instantly as well. I put the gun up and signaled for the guys to come down. I ran over and picked up Lola. I carried her in my arms back to the truck. I held her on my lap until we made it back to the clubhouse. The bag of money I had thrown at him was just a bag of trash. We wouldn't have actually brought the money with us, since we had no intention to give it back.

WHEN WE MADE IT BACK, I put Lola in the car and David drove us home. I took her inside and laid her on my bed while I ran her a bath. It was really hard to look at her face and to see the damage that they'd done to her without breaking down. When the water was perfect enough for her to get in, I dropped in a few rose petals and walked back into my room. She was sitting on the edge of the bed and was looking at me.

SHE OPENED her mouth to speak, but quickly closed it. I figured she wanted to talk, but was too tired or in too much pain, so I decided not to bother her about it. I took her clothes off of her and carried her into the bathroom. I sat her down inside of the tub and watched as she winced. I finally had my Lola back, and although she wasn't at her best, I was willing to nurse her back to health.

I WATCHED her as she tried to relearn how to move her arms and legs. It was the saddest thing that I had ever laid eyes on and my heart broke even more, knowing that I was the one who put her in this type of danger. She learned fast. That's how strong she was. Just thinking about how strong she really was made me think back to the different moments that we had shared. Specifically, back to when all of this started.

I KNEW she wanted that kiss as badly as I did, and I knew that the kiss would definitely leave her wanting more. I didn't really have a meeting. I just wanted to leave her on edge. I knew even the strongest, most independent girl couldn't hold herself back. I knew my magic, and it only took a couple of days. I chuckled to myself and walked back to my desk, taking a sip of my coffee while looking out the view of the window. I had everything I wanted in the palm of my hand.

Lola made me feel young again. Being around her took me back to when I was around her age and just starting to discover what love was all about. That was a time when I was wild and adventurous. I had a lot of down time and I could really be myself without any consequences. That was why being with her was such a valuable time for me.

I felt as if she was really the one for me, and that was why it hurt me so much that she would betray me. I felt that, if her feelings were almost the same as mine, she would at least respect my privacy. Whether my email had been left open or not, it wasn't her place to take a look inside.

That whole situation angered me so much, but I just couldn't force myself to be over-the-top upset with her. I knew that showing extreme anger toward her would make me uncomfortable and I couldn't bring myself to hurt her ... that much.

My phone began to ring, disrupting my thoughts and making me slightly irritated. It was a call from David. I answered quickly because it was rare for David to call me in the middle of the day.

"Boss, you're not going to like this." His voice sounded frantic and I almost didn't want to hear what he was going to say next.

"What is it?" I kept my calm. Panicking just as much as he was wouldn't help nothing at that moment.

"That lady who's been chasing you down for years says she's coming after the girl and it's not going to be pretty."

"The girl ...what girl?" I asked in confusion.

"The one you went out with the other night, you know? The one who found out about us," he said. There was a silence on the phone after that as I took a minute to think.

"How'd you figure that out?" I asked.

"She sent me an email from her husband's account he had with us and said these words exactly:"

Dear David and crew,

Since Arsen stole the love of my life from me, I guess I'll have to take something from his as well. That girl—his new arm candy. My daughter has been telling me she's seen them around town together and it's more than just him taking her out to make himself look good. He has feelings for this girl and this is the perfect time for me to come in and make my move. I just hope you guys get a hold of her before I do.

"Arsen." Lola called out, breaking my train of thought.

"Yes, my love?" I got on my knees in front of the tub, willing to do whatever she asked.

"Why did you kill my best friend?" She looked over at me with wide eyes. Her knees were pulled up to her chest.

. . .

"Who told you that?" I asked, wondering how she found out.

"I heard the gunshots, and when they took me out of the building, I saw her laying there. Dead. Her mother said you did it." She sniffled and I saw her eyes begin to tear up. "You killed her and her father."

"Lola ..." I started, and honestly, I didn't know how to finish.

"You took her father away from her and you took her away from me! How do I know if I'm next?" She tried to speak louder, but I could tell it was putting a strain on her throat.

"Lola, I would never hurt you a day in my life," I spoke.

"Prove it," she said quietly. "Don't hurt anyone else close to me, please."

"Anything for you." I nodded.

"Now tell me why? Why did you kill her? Why did you kill her father?" She looked down at the water.

"Well, her father was stealing money from us and giving it to other gangs who were against us. He was one of our best members and the entire time he was setting us up." I lathered a washcloth with soap and started to clean her up. "As far as Anabella, her and her mother were plotting on hurting you in order to get back at me"

She looked up at me in disbelief.

"There's no need for me to lie. The situation is over now." I continued to clean her. "Your best friend was plotting against you."

Things got quiet really fast. As I washed over her body with the cloth, the only sound between us was the light movements of the bath water. I grabbed the bottle of strawberry shampoo and began washing her hair. She sat there, staring into space. More than likely, she thinking about what I had just told her.

I finished washing her up and sat there. I reached for the drain to let the water out, but she grabbed my hand, stopping me.

"Can I stay in here a little longer?" she whispered. I nodded and still drained the water.

"Anything you want, my love. Let me just run you some fresh water." I slightly smiled, trying to make her comfortable and ran her some more warm water.

. . .

"I'm going to go take a shower in your room, if that's okay?"

She nodded and I got up to leave. Before I left, I grabbed my phone, turning on some soft music at a low volume and sitting it on the sink for her to listen to. Maybe the music would help her calm down. She'd been in the same position since she got in.

As I cracked the door, I saw her relax her body. She pulled her legs down from her chest and stretched her arms out. She lowered her body into the tub, so that the water touched her neck. It made me smile that she felt at home.

I grabbed a fresh towel and a pair of sweats to wear to bed and headed off into her room. I took off my clothes and got into the shower. I hadn't had a good shower since the day Lola had gone missing.

I made sure the water was hot and the shower was steamy. That way I could really relax and become one with my thoughts. I began washing over my body slowly, being sure not to miss a spot. I washed my hair, then stood under the water for a few minutes, soaking up the heat before I went back into the chill air of my bedroom.

When I got out, I dried off my body and threw on my sweats. I took a deep breath and walked back to my room. Upon entering, my eyes fell upon Lola, who was in my bed, laying on her side. It looked like she had a gown on. She must've gotten it out of her room when I was in the shower.

. . .

She looked so peaceful. Just when I was about to turn to go sleep in her room, I heard her voice.

"Arsen," she whispered.

"Yes, angel?" I asked, walking over to the edge of her bed.

"Stay," she commanded in a light voice.

"You sure?"

"Yes. Please don't leave me. Sleep with me, please," she whined.

"All right." I climbed into bed next to her and turned off the desk lamp, which was the only light on.

The moonlight shone inside of the windows as Lola turned to face me. She cuddled up to me and I wrapped my arm around her. I was so glad to have her back next to me.

THE END

SIGN UP TO RECEIVE FREE BOOKS

Sign Up to Receive Free E-Books and Audiobook Codes.

Would you like to read **The Unexpected Nanny, Dirty Little Virgin** and **other romance books** for free?

You can sign up to receive these free e-books and audiobooks by typing this link into your browser:

https://www.steamyromance.info/free-books-and-audiobooks-hot-and-steamy/

Or this one:

https://www.steamyromance.info/the-unexpected-nanny-free/

PREVIEW OF THE SURGEON'S SECRETS

A Bad Boy Billionaire Romance

By Celeste Fall & Michelle Love

Blurb

Samantha

Dr. Damon Chase just saved my life, going over my doctor's head to perform a life-saving surgery. He's taken me from wondering if I'll die soon to looking forward to my life, and I'm falling for him fast and hard. There are just two problems.

The first one is that the medical ethics board won't look kindly on a senior cardiologist sleeping with any of his patients, let alone a college student just over half his age. The second is that Damon is a man full of secrets. I can sense it. But what can they be? And how can I get him past them, so that I can have him in my arms?

Damon

I'm stuck on a sweet, young thing I saved on the table, even though I know it could get me in a world of trouble. Samantha North. Every time she makes eyes at me, I want to do something about it ...in as many ways and as many positions as she likes. We're both alone in the world—and I've grown tired of that. I'd consider it more than worth it to risk my professional reputation to have her in my bed and in my life. If that was the only problem, anyway.

But back home in London, I had another life ...a life full of secrets. But abandoning the life of crime that I once led has made me some serious enemies—and that's about to catch up with me. If they find out about Samantha, her life will be in danger. And if that happens, that oath I took to do no harm is going right out the window.

CHAPTER 1

Samantha

"Are you sure Dr. Carpenter can't at least take a message?" I plead with the receptionist on the other end of the line. "I know he says that the Verapamil takes some time to take effect, but it's been a week and a half, and I can barely make it to classes."

"I'm sorry," the receptionist says in a bland tone that tells me she couldn't care less. "But his voicemail box is full. He should be back from lunch at 3 PM. If you can catch him before we close, he should be able to advise you."

"So ...when do you close?" I'm trying not to get upset. The pounding in my chest will only get worse if I do.

I try to distract myself by glancing around at the little stand of trees that surrounds me as I sit on a bench at the edge of campus. I started getting dizzy and sick again just walking up a slight incline for a quarter mile, and it scared me.

"We close at 4 PM." She sounds disgusted—whether with me, her boss, or her job, I'm not sure.

"Thank you." I wish that I could reach through the phone

and strangle her. Instead, I take a deep, slow breath and struggle to keep my cool as I hang up.

I have to sit there a while as the stress sends a fresh wave of dizziness through me. I'm barely holding back my panic, which I know will only add to the problem. Even then, a few tears roll down my cheeks.

The pills aren't doing anything. I need real help and expertise. Not that cheap doctor who just throws drugs at everything!

The problem started six months ago: bouts of painfully fast and sometimes irregular heartbeats, with dizziness, weakness, and exhaustion. Dr. Campbell keeps trying different pills on me. But even high doses of beta blockers barely put a dent in my symptoms.

My scholarship includes student medical coverage. Unfortunately, it's low-bidder garbage, and Campbell is the only cardiologist in town who takes it. He and his receptionist team have a habit of treating me like dirt when I can least handle it.

Just calm down, Sam. It will get worse if you don't.

This is getting humiliating. In my freshman year I was zipping around campus on my bike like it was nothing. Now and again I would feel a little dizzy, but I was used to that. I've dealt with it my whole life.

Then the attacks started happening. The first time, I was just coming down for breakfast in the dorm cafeteria, ready to face my very last day of finals in my freshman year. I remember walking downstairs to the dorm lobby and stopping short, growing suddenly dizzy as my heart pounded violently.

It's gotten worse since then. Now I shuffle around like an old woman and spend too much of the money I earn at my part-time job on cab fare to get home. I even had to quit my weekly swims.

I can't even soak in the hot tub anymore—and that used to be my number one way to relax. But, now, the hot water will make me even dizzier, as it drives up my already overactive heart rate.

Dr. Campbell claimed recently that I'm not getting better because I'm not taking my meds. I had to get a test to prove to him that my bloodstream is full of the damn drugs; they just aren't doing shit. His response was to try a different set of drugs, which, again, do very little.

I get up and lift my art bag, an old, gray, canvas messenger bag covered in spatters of oil paint, smears of pastel and chalk, and smudges of charcoal. I've had it since I was twelve—one of the few gifts I ever got growing up in the foster system. Right now, it feels like it's filled with bricks.

My final class of the day is at six—a night studio where all I have to do is stand there, paint, and try not to fall over. I don't even have to wrestle any of the big canvases today—it's all five-minute speed sessions on paper. I'll grab a light meal, drink something without any caffeine in it, go up the hill, and throw on my smock.

I'm feeling better after a meal and some fluids. I keep trying the doctor until four, but he makes no effort to return my call. "He has other patients," the receptionist says without apology, while my heart beats so fast and hard it nauseates me.

I wonder if this callous bitch of a receptionist has ever gotten really sick in her life. If things keep getting worse, I'm going to end up in the emergency room again. I already have a huge bill from last month that I can't pay, and the prospect of facing yet another one makes my heart beat even faster.

I agonize over that possibility while I sit on that bench and call Campbell twice more before his office closes. Tears start running down my cheeks after I hang up the second time, and I wipe them away sternly. *Enough of that.*

I didn't get this far by giving up or feeling sorry for myself. I'll find some way to survive this, just like I survived foster care, public school, and getting my ass into college on a full ride. But as I get up and start walking at a painful snail's pace toward the student center, I'm scared to death.

I spend a lot of my time on campus alone. I'm kind of used to it. In school, I was the kid with no parents, who went home to an institutional cot and food that was marginally worse than the stuff in the dorm cafeterias.

Making friends is a new skill for me. Here, at least, classes are so huge that nobody notices that I'm recycling through the same half-dozen outfits every week. But it doesn't make approaching people any easier.

Still, when I get back that evening, completely drained and with paint smudges on my hands, I exchange greetings with a few people on my way up to my dorm room. The guard station and a lot of the dorm doors are decorated for Christmas—mostly cheap, printed, paper decorations, tinsel garlands, and sometimes a string of colored or silver LED lights. The bulletin board on my floor is full of seasonal party announcements.

I try to ignore them and just make it to my door. The sight of them tends to leave me depressed.

I was lucky enough to have been assigned one of the rare single rooms. The room is tiny and plain, but it's the first private room I have ever had in my life, so I refuse to complain.

It's not even eight, and I know that if I sleep now, chances are I'll end up getting up at some weird hour. But I can barely keep my eyes open, so I don't really care. It's bedtime.

I leave my bag and clothes in a pile, pull on a huge, purple t-shirt and shorts, and crawl under the covers, barely remembering to set my phone on the bedside table. If I sleep long enough, the pain in my chest may actually go away for a while.

I wake up hours later to total darkness. I feel like a huge weight has dropped onto my chest. My heart is galloping like I'm running a race, making me dizzy and sick. I gasp and try to sit up, but it hurts too much. *Oh my God, am I dying?*

I flail for my phone and almost knock it off the small table before managing to grab it. Every single heartbeat pounds in my head, my chest burns and aches, and the sides of my neck hurt, like my veins are going to burst.

I manage to dial for help, but everything after that gets vaguer and vaguer. I give my name, location, and information about my heart condition, but it sounds like my voice is coming from far off, as if someone else is in control of it. It feels like I'm drifting further and further from my dorm room, out over a black sea, where the pounding of my heart is all I can hear.

I hang on through sheer force of will as the 911 dispatcher keeps me on the phone and tries to help me stay conscious. The whine of sirens echoes toward me from afar. Then, the darkness closes over my head, and I hear rather than see my phone drop to the floor.

CHAPTER 2

Damon

I'm dreaming about the night of the heist again when my phone goes off and drags me straight up from the depths of sleep. One minute I'm jumping into a bank vault while the explosion drops the entire building around me, and the next, my eyes are opening in my posh Chicago penthouse and I'm fine. Except, of course, that my phone woke me up at three in the fucking morning, and who wants to deal with that?

I check the text and immediately sit up. "Shit."

There's a college girl in the ER with some kind of severe heart issue. Her cardiologist isn't returning his calls, and since I'm the cardio man on call tonight, it's time for me to hop to it. I leap out of bed and head for my closet, grumbling curses the whole time, but ready to get my game on.

The *new* game. The one where I'm saving lives instead of chasing cash and trouble back in London. New game—new name, new identity, new life. And I have work to do.

I text the desk nurse back as I take the elevator down from the penthouse. *How are her vitals?*

She gets back to me quickly. *Rapid, irregular heartbeat, with dizziness and pain in her temples, chest, and the sides of her neck. She's diagnosed with congenital arrhythmia and tachycardia, the latter presumed to be anxiety-related. She's on a calcium blocker and a sedative.*

Arrhythmia? There are many kinds of arrhythmia, and it doesn't bode well that her doctor hasn't put an exact diagnosis on her chart. *What's her electrophysiology study say about it?*

She hasn't had one. Her insurance barely covers the specialist, and her doctor wouldn't do it pro bono. She would have had to pay for it out of pocket.

"Which, of course, she can't fucking do because she's a dirt-poor college student. Fuck," I mumble under my breath. I step out of the elevator into the garage and head for my black Prowler. "I hate for-profit medicine so damned much."

I slide into the driver's seat and text back. *All right. Stop the calcium blockers, keep her calm, and introduce the following into her IV cocktail.* I give a list of three drugs I know they have on hand. *We're going to need to do that study as soon as she is stable enough.*

We'll get it done. ETA?

Ten minutes, barring traffic. Whose name is on the chart as her specialist? I have my suspicions, but I still grit my teeth when she confirms them.

Campbell.

"Fuck." Adrian Campbell is the worst, most negligent cardiologist in Chicago. The two of us are colleagues, but every time I run into him at a conference, I want to punch him in the face.

I've never met a man who mixes arrogance with incompetence as thoroughly as Campbell. He always has at least three malpractice cases pending, and he's killed more patients than he's saved. That girl is as good as dead if she stays in his hands.

Going to have to do something about that, I think to myself.

I put my phone down and strap in, then start the engine and

go roaring out into the street. It's chilly out; early December hasn't put snow on the ground yet, but I keep an eye on the road, wary of black ice.

Chicago on the cusp of winter reminds me a bit of London, though the streets tend to be wider and more organized, and the weather's more changeable. Bits of rain spatter my windshield, making tiny, distracting taps against the glass. The streets aren't quite deserted, even at this hour; a few people fight the wind in flapping raincoats as I drive by.

It's Christmas season again, which usually leaves me a bit melancholy. It's not like I can call my family back in London, let alone see them. The colored lights and the wreaths on the lampposts are just another reminder that I'm out on my own here in the States.

I speed where I can on the way to the hospital, but keep it sane. I'm not some twenty-something idiot behind the wheel of my first sports car any longer. I just feel a strange urgency with this particular patient, maybe because she's young.

Nineteen-years-old with heart problems. *What a fucking bad hand she has been dealt.* Barely old enough to vote and she's dealing with an issue most folks don't have to face until their sixties or beyond.

I make my way into the staff parking section and ease the Prowler into my space, making sure to lock up before hurrying over to the ER. My foot slips slightly on a patch of ice outside the entrance, and I bite back a curse. I rarely swear on hospital grounds.

"Morning, Dr. Chase. You're in early," Tom, the security guard, greets me.

I give him a distracted nod hello. "Emergency. Some nineteen-year-old girl's down with a congenital heart problem. Time to pop in and roll up my sleeves."

"Nineteen? Damn. Well, I'm sure you'll be able to help her." He smiles and buzzes me in, and I hurry through.

It's a slow day in the emergency department. The waiting room, with its slowly blinking lights and silver tinsel tree, only has two people, and though every treatment room is full, only one of them has nurses rushing in and out. I feel my heart sink when I see them scurry. *You didn't code while I was on my way, did you, darling?*

"Dr. Chase!" One of the senior nurses, a skinny, bespectacled, older woman named Sarah, bustles toward me with an armful of files. "Thanks for coming so quickly. She's down here."

This is the only place in the world where a guy gets thanked for that. I keep my filthy thoughts to myself as I follow her to the curtained-off room for my first look at Samantha North.

"We've got her stabilized. She's been coming in and out of consciousness. We're prepping for the study now." We go in past the curtain, and I blink down at my new patient.

Shit. The girl's half my age, vulnerable, likely terrified, and very much needs for me to focus on my work right now. But as I walk over to the bed and look down at her, I realize that focusing is going to be a bit difficult.

She's a complete knockout. On the tall side, with milky skin, wavy, red hair, full lips, and a body that looks hot even in a hospital gown. Her breasts are half-uncovered so we can attach the sensors and defibrillate quickly if we must, and I have to tear my eyes away.

For fuck's sake, Damon, get your mind out of her panties and set to work on saving her fucking life! I look over her vitals, then check her chart once Sarah hands it over. "Question. Is her heart rate going back up no matter what drug is being used?"

"Looks like it, yes." She looks over my shoulder at the chart, then turns the page and points to the EKG readouts. "Sedatives helped some and beta blockers helped some. The calcium blockers didn't seem to do anything at all."

"It could be worse than that. Some arrhythmias respond negatively to calcium blockers. That's why I had you stop them. The study will show us more of what is going on."

I purse my lips and then hand the chart back to Sarah as I go on. "It's possible that she may need laparoscopic surgery before this is over. I'll drive the scope myself. See if they can keep the operating room on standby after they run the study?"

She smiles and nods, seeming relieved. How many times had she tried to call that damned idiot, Campbell, before she gave up and called me? Not too many, I hope.

The poor girl stays unconscious through the entire test; just as well, since it involves threading a scope into her circulatory system. The procedure will only leave her with some soreness and a small entry wound, but the very thought of it gives a lot of patients the shudders. Still, it will save her from open-heart surgery, unless everything in her heart is completely fucked up.

I look over her chart as we wait for the results and am surprised to see an insert from Family Services from only two years ago. Yet another reminder that I shouldn't be staring at her tits, especially openly.

No family. Grew up in foster care. Started off life as Baby Doe after being found in an auto wreck that destroyed her presumed parents, but somehow left her without a bruise.

No record of any distant relatives or foster parents. The facility she was in sent her to the same pediatrician until she aged out of the system, and to my relief, they've sent a copy of her medical records. Dr. Marsh did a much better job in tracking her health issues than the student clinic or, of course, Dr. Campbell.

Reported incidents of light-headedness back through the age of ten. Believed to be anxiety-related, but she has neither a formal anxiety diagnosis nor a diagnosis of PTSD. *And yet doctors keep treating her for anxiety anyway, telling her that what she's been feeling since she was a kid is all in her head.*

If there's one thing I hate more than incompetent doctors, it's prejudiced doctors. The sort who go in assuming they know what's what because their patient is a fat guy, or a smoker, or a young woman. Every body is different, and though certain types tend toward certain conditions, diagnosis and treatment are never one-size-fits-all.

The girl, who's now resting in a nest of wires, sensors, and tubes, her heart still going too damned fast, needs precision as much as she needs empathy. I can offer both, though I can already tell that this one's going to wreck me if she passes. Occupational hazard; I accept it just as I once accepted that I wouldn't live past the age of thirty-five.

Half an hour later, I have my answers. I want to talk to the girl before we actually go in and fix the matter, so she knows what is going on. But I'm determined to do the surgery tonight, before Campbell can make any more of a mess of this.

I have them lower the sedation level so she has a better chance of waking up quickly and then have them watch her until she does.

Not long after, they summon me back to her bedside. I walk in, putting on the best fucking bedside manner I can muster before dawn and my first cup of tea. "Miss North? I'm Dr. Chase, the on-call cardiologist."

Her eyes widen as she takes me in. Even in the midst of her terror, I catch an ember of something I didn't expect in her expression. Time enough to discuss that later, though. "Hi," she manages in a breathless voice.

"Hi there. I'm very sorry about meeting you under these circumstances, but I do have some good news for you, if you feel up to hearing it." I catch myself smiling a bit too much and dial it back, chastising myself.

"Good news is pretty welcome about now. I'm guessing I'm ...out of danger, then?" She forces a tiny, brave smile.

I'm arrested by it briefly, then cough into my fist, trying to cover my lapse. "Yes, well, we performed the test that Campbell neglected to give you, and I can now explain to you what is going on in your heart and how we are going to fix it."

"Oh?" She makes the mistake of trying to sit up and almost immediately stops, wincing in pain at the effort. "Damn."

"Well, we haven't patched you up yet, so don't get too impatient to jump out of bed," I joke with her gently. She offers that brave, charming, little smile again.

"So ...what's wrong with me?" Her voice only shakes a little.

"It's called Wolff-Parkinson-White Syndrome. As you told our nurse that you suspected, it is not treated with calcium channel blockers, such as Verapamil. In fact, they're contraindicated. They can make the situation worse."

She's got one hell of a malpractice suit to bring against that bastard Campbell for his misdiagnosis and mistreatment of a life-threatening disease. I am so sick of his shit that I decide to help her if she'll accept the offer. "We took you off the drugs, and I want you to stop taking them when you get home."

She nods quickly. "Yes, doctor. Should I get rid of them?"

"No. Keep them and decide whether you want to take legal action once you are feeling better. You can use them to support your case, since he put you on something that probably made things worse." I look at her and feel a stab of alarm as her eyes tear up.

"I knew it," she said in a shaky voice. "I knew something was wrong. He and his staff weren't listening."

"I'm afraid that Dr. Campbell is somewhat well known for that. Unfortunately, those on campus health insurance don't exactly have their pick of specialists." She nods, still teary-eyed, and before I can stop myself, I reach out and put a hand on her shoulder.

She stops shaking at once and the waterworks slow. She looks up at me and smiles sadly. "So what does this syndrome do, and how do we stop it?"

"Well, the short explanation is that the heart has nodes that send electrical impulses through it and tell it when to contract. You happen to have too many of those nodes. They fire at their own rates, and for much of your life, they were likely firing almost in sync with one another. That means they were telling your heart to contract at the same time.

"That means for most of your life, your heart beat like a normal heart. Sometimes the two signals would get out of sync and you would get dizzy, but they likely always went back into sync with one another.

"But, somehow, this year, the two signals went out of sync, and now each one is telling the heart to beat at different times. And your heart is beating extra fast and unevenly to keep up with what the signals tell it to do."

I watch her face as she struggles to digest what—despite my simplifying it as much as possible—was a standard-issue doctorly info-dump. She looks thoughtful, then raises her head to look at me.

"Okay. Thank you for figuring that out for me. Now ...how do we fix it?"

CHAPTER 3

Samantha

I'm about to trust my life to the hottest doctor I have ever seen—and I've had my share of medical emergencies. Holy crap, though, this guy ... Looking at him almost takes my mind off the fact that he's going to thread a weird robotic tentacle through my veins.

He's got some kind of British accent—more working-class than Oxford—but despite that, he looks Mediterranean. His wavy hair is almost jet black, and he has it pulled back into a short ponytail at his nape. He has olive skin, liquid brown eyes, and a Roman nose above a wide, well-shaped mouth.

He's tall and broad-shouldered under that white lab coat, and even in my drugged haze, I can't help but notice that he moves like a panther. But most of all, he's got me captivated because he has the answers, because he cares enough to do his job right, and because he's about to fix my problem instead of just throwing pills at it.

The surgical theater is small, and computer screens and equipment dominate one of its walls. I lie on the table while the anesthesiologist prepares my deep sedation. Meanwhile, Dr. Chase is walking me through what's going to happen next.

"Radio frequency ablation is not a long process. We already went in once to run the test, and it will be a simple matter to go in again. I'd estimate half an hour to go in with the laparoscope, and then we'll monitor you until tomorrow."

"That's it? You're telling me that I could be well by tomorrow morning." I can't believe what I'm hearing. No more pills? No more dizzy spells? No more being afraid my damn heart will give out?

"Well, more or less. You'll need to take it easy for about a week after everything you have been through, but normally, this is an outpatient procedure. We'll cause the extra electrical node to stop sending signals using radio waves, and then you're done." He checks my vitals, then makes a few notes. "Right, well, I should go get ready. See you when you wake up!"

The anesthesiologist, a tiny Filipino woman with graying roots, smiles at me and gives Dr. Chase a nod. "All right, sweetie, I'm going to put this in your IV port, and it's going to make you very relaxed. You won't actually remember anything afterward."

"So, like when I got my wisdom teeth out?" I'm nervous, but this is going to happen; it has to happen. And pretty soon I'll be too high to care about what's going on anyway.

"Like twilight sleep, yes." She takes a syringe and slowly empties the milky fluid inside into my IV line. "And here we are. Now, I'd like you to count back from one hundred for me."

"Okay," I say, feeling a different sort of dizziness. A warm rush seems to be riding through my veins. "One hundred ...ninety-nine ...ninety-eight ...ninety-seven ...."

"Uh?" I wake up in a small recovery room, feeling a little bit of pain on the inside of one thigh. I'm sleepy and a little queasy, and the pain is completely gone except for that ache in my upper thigh. I lie there blinking, shocked by the loss of time and memory, even though I was warned.

My heart is beating slowly as the monitor beeps along. It picks up as I notice it, but not by much. I don't hurt; I take a huge breath and my chest doesn't ache. I have no trouble filling my lungs with air, something I haven't been able to do in a long time.

Intrigued, I press two fingers against my pulse to double check. It feels ...normal. Even. It's not racing at all.

Holy crap. He got it! Dr. Unexpected British Hottie actually fixed me!

All I can do is lie there and stare at the ceiling for a while, grateful tears leaking down the sides of my face. I'm not going to die. *I'm going to be okay.*

And I have Dr. Chase to thank for it.

The door opens, and I look up—expecting a nurse—but it's him, and he's smiling like he's trying not to gloat. "How are you feeling?" he asks, his eyes twinkling.

"Much better," I breathe. "Is that ...is that it?"

"Once you're discharged, I'll want to see you in my office in about a week. I'll make sure you're given an appointment card with directions." He puts his stethoscope in his ears and warms the business end with his hand before laying it above my left breast.

He smiles after a moment. "Deep breaths?" I oblige, and he withdraws, nodding. "Yeah, I'm ninety-eight percent certain that this is sewn up. As is your leg, which may be sore for a few days."

"Thank you, doctor," I say, managing to stop my eyes from leaking again. "I don't know what I would have done ...." I trail off, because I *do* know. I would have died, and it would have been at least partly Campbell's fault.

The thought sobers me a little, but not because it scares me.

Now that I can think beyond the possibility of dying, I'm thinking about the possibility of *suing*.

"Don't think of it. You'll be fine now if you look after yourself for a few days." His voice goes from professional to almost tender, distracting me from my growing anger.

I sigh and sit up easily this time. He reaches over and adjusts the backrest for me. The little bit of extra care makes me smile, but it feels unnecessary—I already feel better than I have in months.

"I have to think about it, though," I admit. "Because I'm gonna go sue the crap out of Dr. Campbell once I'm well enough."

He chuckles, and there's a dark gleam in his eyes now, intriguing me. I stare back at him, tilting my head, and he finally says, "You know, I'm absolutely done with that idiot as well. Would you like some help with lawsuit preparations?"

My heart leaps. It has plenty of reasons to leap—he has healed it, he wants to help me even though he doesn't have to, and ...he *is* hot as a Chicago summer. Smiling, I reply, "I'd like that."

CHAPTER 4

Damon

I can't wipe the smile off my face by the time I make my way back home. Saving anyone's life is always one for the win column, but Samantha ...well. That girl is special.

Too damn young for me, but I'm still pretty smitten. I know I'm offering help because a part of me just wants to keep her around for a bit longer. And thanks to pure happenstance, I know that she wants to keep me around as well.

The funny part is I know she is quite interested, but I have doubts about taking advantage of that knowledge. I'm not supposed to know she's interested—that information slipped out while she was drugged. She got very ...chatty ...while sedated. Of course, she won't remember it now.

. . .

"Oh, wow, you're so hot! Are you single? Do you want to go out with me now that I'm not gonna die?"

It was absolutely adorable. The nurses and my colleague, Dr. Pinoy, all giggled, and I grinned and acted embarrassed and awkward—all the while hoping no one noticed that I was hard as hell. And my expression made my staff giggle more.

But I didn't say no—only that I would think about it. And I am thinking about it as I drive home ...a lot.

Being a doctor, I see a lot more of my patients than members of pretty much any other profession. Not just their guts or the insides of their veins, but more skin than most people would prefer—including me, sometimes. And tending to Samantha, I saw quite a bit.

A perfect breast that I had to ignore, the curve of her inner thigh as I inserted the catheter, and the smooth slope of her belly as the nurses adjusted her draping. Her obvious sex appeal was a distraction, but I fought it off and did the work to save her life, without looking at or touching her inappropriately.

At any other time, the sight of the flawless, silk-skinned globe of her breast would have driven me to at least try flirting with her. There was no ring on her finger. There was no worried boyfriend in the lobby, and she had even asked me out.

. . .

ONLY PROBLEM IS, I'm her doctor. I can end up before the medical board on ethics charges if I'm fucking her and treating her at the same time. Even once I'm done treating her—which will be in a week—it could cost me my position. If it gets out, anyway.

I HAVE an excuse to see her, but not an excuse to sleep with her. Just the thought of sleeping with her drives me a bit crazy. Last time I felt this turned on by a woman was years ago, with Molly back in London—in fact, Samantha heats me up even more.

NOT GOING to do a thing about it unless she's vocal about being into it, though. Sometimes what a lady is open to trying when she's drunk on some inebriant is not what she's ready for when she's sober. I may be a rogue and a bastard, but not when it comes to women—or my patients.

THERE'S something bleak about driving back home during the morning commute hours. I've done it many times over the years, usually because I was in on an ER consult or emergency surgery. And before that, there was all the times with my crew back home in London.

I CHECK the clock on the dash: it's 8 AM. "Damn my luck, none of the pubs are open." I hate coming home with my cock hard and my stomach empty.

I COULD HAVE USED a hot meal and a pint or two at Monk's, but

I'll have to settle for ordering something up. At least a lot of delivery places in Chicago do morning hours. I am, and have always been, a disaster in the kitchen.

I GET BACK to the penthouse and start looking up pizza places. Chicago-style pizza is, without doubt, the best in the world. I order a large, all-meat, extra cheese—the sort I'd nag my patients about if it wasn't usually their sedentary lifestyle that was fucking them up anyway. I'll burn off that beast of a pizza in the gym between today and tomorrow, which is about how long it will take me to finish it.

I pour brandy into my tea, throw a dollop of honey into it, and settle into an overstuffed, brown, velvet chair in my living room to await my delivery. I've already told the doorman to receive the pie and how much to tip. I'll save my bottle of IPA to drink with my pizza.

MY SCHEDULE'S off and I could use a nap, but I'm lucky to have nothing else going with work today until this evening. The only possible reason they'll call me in is if they need another emergency heart consult or fix, and that doesn't happen every night. I'm not needed for the average heart attack or gunshot wound.

THE PIZZA PLACE is six blocks off, and they know how much I tip, so I get my pie in well under half an hour. I'm setting it on the table and opening the box lid for that first whiff of scented steam when my phone goes off.

ANNOYED, I scoop it up and see from the screen that it's Dr.

Campbell's office. "Oh, hell," I growl, already annoyed with the man, and especially so for his popping up now. Taking a deep breath, I force myself back into my doctor's demeanor and answer the call.

"This is Dr. Chase. May I help you?"

"Dr. Chase." Campbell has one of those dull, nasal, whiny voices that never seem to change pitch much. "I understand that you have taken over the care of one of my patients."

I can tell he's annoyed, even past his bland demeanor. It's all I can do not to grin. *Yeah, I did, and she's going to sue your sad ass, and I'm fucking well going to help her.* "I'm sorry, could you be a bit more specific?"

The truth is—and he damn well knows it—that I am on-call at the ER four nights a week because I spend so much time cleaning up Campbell's messes. His poor suturing, inability to properly direct nurses, and corner-cutting have often left me fighting for the lives of his patients.

I have even lost a few, which I despise him for, because all but one could have been saved if Campbell had done his job.

"Her name is Samantha North. Age nineteen, height five-foot-seven, red hair. You performed an ablation on her this morning at six."

Funny how the fucker can rattle off details about her with no problem when he's feeling territorial, but he barely did a thing to help her when she needed it. "Oh yeah, the college girl who turned up with Wolff-Parkinson-White."

There is a long pause. "I did not make that diagnosis."

"Right, well, that's because there was no electrophysiology study done on her. Otherwise, I'm presuming that you wouldn't have had her on the Verapamil, since it's contraindicated for her condition." I am smiling a hard, predatory smile that makes my cheeks hurt.

Fucker. You and I both know you're incompetent and don't care to improve. I came up out of the gutters of London a complete miscreant, and I care about your patients more than you do ... all right, especially if they're hot. I'm not anywhere near perfect, and I know it.

He pauses again. I almost wish I could see his face. Finally, he coughs. "I see. So the ablation was done on an emergency basis?"

"That *was* what they summoned me to the ER for, yes." It's like he doesn't even realize how much of a fool he is currently making of himself. I wonder in a fit of charity if he's had his coffee yet.

"You realize that you are not in the system for her student insurance, so why did your assistant schedule her for the follow-up consult?"

I wince. I hate how much the damn nurses gossip and how far and fast that gossip spreads. I'm sure it's one of his receptionists funneling the information to him, as no one else can stand him.

"Nora scheduled her because I'm finishing what I started. I'll be taking her on pro bono. You'll no longer have to worry about anything to do with her." My voice is warm, friendly, and reassuring. I don't want him suspecting that I'm going to be helping Samantha bring down a load of karma on him.

"Oh! Well, fine. If you feel like taking one of my charity cases off of my hands, I'm not going to complain."

Charity case? That pisses me off for some reason, and I bite back a response. Forcing myself to calm down, I smile again and keep my tone so sweetly pleasant that he'll miss the bald-faced lie. "Yes, this should be the last you hear about her heart issues, except for a note for your files."

. . .

"Thank you for the reassurance," he says obliviously and hangs up.

"That and the fat fucking lawsuit you'll be facing once I help that girl get everything together," I swear as I set my phone back down. *I can't wait to see his face when we nail him on this together.*

I'm good and angry when I go back to my tea, which has cooled too much. I take a few tepid swallows and scowl, thinking hard about what I will need to do to help Samantha build a case. But before I can grab myself some pizza, I catch a glint of light out of the corner of my eye.

My head swivels on instinct and my eyes fix on the high-rise parking structure across the street. Its top floor is level with my penthouse, giving me an easy, if distant, view of it. There's a man standing at the front edge of the parking structure, up against the railing, facing me.

All I can tell about him is that he's big, even taller than me, and dressed in dark colors. I catch that gleam from him again, but before I can go for my telescope or the binoculars hanging over the mantel, he turns and starts walking away. He walks with a slight limp, and I'm left wondering if it was just coincidence or something else.

If you want to continue reading this story, you can get your copy from your favorite vendor by searching for the title:

The Surgeon's Secrets

A Bad Boy Billionaire Romance

You can also find the e-book version by typing this link in your computer's browser:

https://www.hotandsteamyromance.com/products/the-surgeon-s-secrets-a-bad-boy-billionaire-romance

OTHER BOOKS BY THIS AUTHOR

Saving Her Rescuer: A Billionaire & A Virgin Romance

I was just trying to get away from my crazy ex for the weekend when I ended up in a giant pileup on the highway up to Gore Mountain.

https://geni.us/SavingHerRescuer

∽

Sensual Sounds: A Rockstar Ménage

Lust. Lies. Double lives.

The rock and roll industry is full of people who are looking out for themselves and willing to do anything to rise to the top.

https://www.hotandsteamyromance.com/collections/frontpage/products/sensual-sounds-a-rockstar-menage

∽

On the Run: A Secret Baby Romance

Murder. Lies. Fraud. Just another day in the lives of billionaires and women on the run.

https://www.hotandsteamyromance.com/collections/frontpage/products/on-the-run-a-secret-baby-romance

∽

The Dirty Doctor's Touch: A Billionaire Doctor Romance

I am a master. An elitist. I am at the top of my field, and I know what I am doing.

https://www.hotandsteamyromance.com/collections/frontpage/products/the-dirty-doctor-s-touch-a-billionaire-doctor-romance

The Hero She Needs: A Single Daddy Next Door Romance

He's the only man I've ever wanted...

https://www.hotandsteamyromance.com/collections/frontpage/products/the-hero-she-needs-a-single-daddy-next-door-romance

You can find all of my books here:

Hot and Steamy Romance

https://www.hotandsteamyromance.com

ABOUT THE AUTHOR

Mrs. Love writes about smart, sexy women and the hot alpha billionaires who love them. She has found her own happily ever after with her dream husband and adorable 6 and 2 year old kids.
Currently, Michelle is hard at work on the next book in the series, and trying to stay off the Internet.
"Thank you for supporting an indie author. Anything you can do, whether it be writing a review, or even simply telling a fellow reader that you enjoyed this. Thanks

Facebook
    facebook.com/HotAndSteamyRomance

Instagram
    instagram.com/michellesromance

COPYRIGHT

©Copyright 2020 by Michelle Love - All rights Reserved

In no way is it legal to reproduce, duplicate, or transmit any part of this document in either electronic means or in printed format. Recording of this publication is strictly prohibited and any storage of this document is not allowed unless with written permission from the publisher. All rights are reserved. Respective authors own all copyrights not held by the publisher.

www.ingramcontent.com/pod-product-compliance
Lightning Source LLC
LaVergne TN
LVHW021657060526
838200LV00050B/2395

9781648080548